THE

COHEN!

THE OC

by Aury Wallington
Based on the characters created by Josh Schwartz

Cohen!

SCHOLASTIC INC.

New York   Toronto   London   Auckland   Sydney
Mexico City   New Delhi   Hong Kong   Buenos Aires

If you purchased this book without a cover, you should be aware that this book is stolen property. It was reported as "unsold and destroyed" to the publisher, and neither the author nor the publisher has received payment for this "stripped book."

No part of this work may be reproduced in whole or in part, stored in a retrieval system, or transmitted in any form or by any means, electronic, mechanical, photocopying, recording, or otherwise, without written permission of the publisher. For more information regarding permission, write to Scholastic Inc., Attention: Permissions Department, 557 Broadway, New York, NY 10012.

ISBN 0-439-74572-1

Copyright © 2006 Warner Bros. Entertainment Inc.
THE O.C. and all related characters and elements are trademarks of and © Warner Bros. Entertainment Inc.
(sO6)
Published by Scholastic Inc.
SCHOLASTIC and associated logos are trademarks and/or registered trademarks of Scholastic Inc.

12 11 10 9 8 7 6 5 4 3 2 1   6 7 8 9 10/0

Printed in the U.S.A.
First printing, March 2006

THE OC

COHEN!

THE OC
2006

"Cohen!" Summer said, pushing Seth off of her and struggling to a sitting position. "Is it your birthday?"

Seth followed Summer's eyes to the nightstand, where he had foolishly propped up the birthday card that arrived in the mail that morning from Florida.

"No," he lied, "the Nana sent that by mistake. She's old and confused. Probably senile."

He tilted Summer's face back toward him and started kissing her again. They had been spending a perfect afternoon lying on top of Seth's bed and kissing while they should have been doing their homework, and Seth was not ready to stop. Especially not for the reason Summer had in mind.

But Summer wasn't going to be deterred. She reached across him and grabbed the goofy Smurf card off of the table. "Yes, it is!" she exclaimed.

Seth groaned and shoved himself up to a sitting position, too, snatching the card away from her. Why hadn't he thought to stick it in a drawer or something before she came over? he asked himself. It's not like he even liked Smurfs. Or was so excited about the check that the Nana sent — seventeen dollars, one for each year — that he needed to have the card on display. He should have just chucked it in the garbage. That way he could have avoided the conversation that he knew was coming — and was already dreading.

"Come on, Summer, can't we just go back to kissing?"

"No!" she said. She put her hand on his chest and gave him a little shove, nabbing the card back.

"I never figured the Nana for a Smurf type," she said, reading the inscription.

"She's not. She's a first-card-she-sees-at-the-drugstore type," Seth said.

"Well, at least she got you a card," Summer said. "I didn't get you anything. And do you know why?"

Seth sighed. Here it came. "Because I didn't tell you it was my birthday."

"Why didn't you?" Summer wailed. She smacked him with the card, then put it back on the nightstand. "When was it? We could have celebrated."

"It's not till this Saturday," Seth told her, "and I don't want to celebrate." He got up from the bed and straightened his Polo shirt, taking a quick glance in the mirror on the bureau to make sure there was no lipstick evidence of their make-out session anywhere on his face. If Summer wasn't going to make out with him anymore, then he might as well go downstairs and get something to drink. He was dying of thirst. Kissing really dried him out.

"That's crazy!" Summer said. "Why not?"

"I never celebrate my birthday," he told her, rubbing a tiny red smudge off the corner of his mouth, "because every time I've ever tried, it's been a disaster."

"Come on," Summer said, "let's have a party. It'll be a blast!" She also stood up, smoothing her clothes and shaking the tangles out of her long, tousled hair.

"No!" Seth said, and to prove his point, he walked out of his room.

"Cohen!" Summer shouted, scrambling after him. "What's the matter with you? Why are you being such a grump?"

"Who's being a grump?" Sandy asked. He came out of his den to see Seth headed down the stairs, Summer at his heels in hot pursuit.

"Hi, Mr. Cohen," Summer said. "I was just telling Seth that he's being impossible about his birthday."

"He told you it was his birthday?" Sandy asked, raising one eyebrow in surprise.

"No!" Summer said, indignant. "And he doesn't want to have a party either."

Sandy chuckled. "Oh, you don't want to try and throw a party for that one," he said. "That's a train wreck waiting to happen."

"Thank you," Seth told his father. He stomped into the kitchen and flung open the refrigerator door, staring bleakly at the contents. "Why don't we ever have any Cokes in here?" he grumbled.

"Because I'm trying to get your birthday off to a bad start," Sandy teased. He pushed aside the carton of orange juice and found two cans of Coke, which he pulled out and handed to the kids.

"I don't get it," Summer said. She popped the top on the can and settled herself on one of the stools at the kitchen counter. "How have they all been so bad?"

"It's the Curse," Seth said, "the Curse of the Cohen."

"I'm afraid he's right," Sandy confirmed, "and it started the day he was born."

THE OC
1989

"It's a boy!" the doctor said, carefully placing the tiny bundle in Kirsten's arms.

"Oh, Sandy, he's beautiful!" Kirsten said through her tears, gazing down at her newborn son.

Sandy moved closer to see. Seth was bright red and wrinkled and would only be beautiful to a monkey. But Sandy smiled at his wife and held out a finger so baby Seth could grab on to it with one tiny, flailing hand.

"He sure is," he agreed. "And look at that grip! This one's gonna be pitching for the Yankees."

Seth snorted. "Sorry to disappoint you, Dad."

Summer punched him on the arm. "Will you let him tell the story?"

"Thank you, Summer," Sandy told her. ". . . And look at that grip," he repeated, with a sidelong glance at Seth. "Give him a pencil and this one's gonna be the next Stan Lee."

Seth couldn't help but grin. "All right. If you're gonna tell the story, at least tell it the way it happened."

"Fine," Sandy said. "As I was saying . . ."

Sandy and Kirsten smiled at each other, and Sandy leaned down to gently kiss his new baby on the top of his head. "I'm never going to let you out of my sight," he whispered.

A nurse bustled into the room and made her way to the young couple. "Do we have a name yet?" she asked them.

Sandy and Kirsten exchanged a look.

"Caleb?" Kirsten said, a question in her voice. "After my father?"

Sandy grimaced. "I thought we'd decided on Jasper."

Now it was Kirsten's turn to make a face. "You decided on that. I was too busy *giving birth* to disagree."

"Well, it's better than — what was it? Cody?"

"Cody's a wonderful name," Kirsten protested.

"Yeah, for a cowboy. Not for a nice Jewish boy from Berkeley."

"Why don't you let me take — Baby Boy Cohen to get him cleaned up," the nurse said, unable to keep the laughter out of her voice. She carefully wrote "Baby Boy Cohen" on a small plastic bracelet that she fastened around the baby's wrist. "This will do until you think up a name," she told them.

She picked up the tiny boy and carried him out of the room, and Sandy and Kirsten squared off. "I thought we'd settled this," Kirsten said.

"No, we'd settled on the name for a girl. And I'll tell you this: No son of mine is going to be named Melinda."

"Melinda!"

Summer laughed so hard that the gulp of Coke

6

she'd just taken came up her nose. "Ow, that hurts!"

"Serves you right," Seth said, glaring at her.

"It was totally worth it," Summer answered, still giggling as she wiped her face with a napkin. "Melinda."

"Tell you what," Sandy said, reaching over to the bed-side table and picking up the pad and pen that lay there, "why don't we each write down three names, and we'll promise right now to choose one of them."

"Okay," Kirsten agreed, taking the sheet of paper he handed her.

They both were silent for a minute as they scribbled their choices, then they finally put their pens down.

"You go first," Kirsten said.

"Okay." Sandy took a deep breath and read his three choices. "Joshua. Levi. Seth."

Kirsten looked down at her paper, then met Sandy's eyes. "Dylan. Max. And . . . Seth."

"Seth Cohen," Sandy said, testing it out. "Senator Seth Cohen."

"I like it," Kirsten said. "Except — Senator?"

"Sorry," Sandy told her. "I meant — *President* Seth Cohen."

"Much better."

She tilted her face up for him to kiss, and they were still smooching when a different nurse walked into the room.

"Hi, I'm Edith, the day-shift nurse," she introduced her-self. "I'll be taking over from here on out. Is there anything I can get you?"

7

"You can bring us our son!" Sandy commanded happily. "It's time for Seth Cohen to begin his assault on the world!"

"I'm bringing our baby home from the hospital today," Kirsten explained, looking amused at Sandy's theatrics. "Can you get Seth Cohen ready to leave?"

"Certainly," Nurse Edith said. A few minutes later, she reappeared with a little blue bundle, so wrapped up in blankets that all they could see was the tip of his nose.

"Here you go," she said, handing him to Kirsten. "You want to make sure he stays nice and warm until you get him home."

Sandy picked up Kirsten's suitcase and shook the nurse's hand. "Thank you for everything," he said. Then he slung his arm around Kirsten's shoulders, and the new family left the hospital.

Sandy carefully steered the car through Berkeley to the small house he and Kirsten were renting. He had spent every spare minute over the last couple of months when he wasn't trying to get his new law practice off the ground putting furniture together for the nursery and painting the walls a bright sunny yellow. The result was a room so cheery that any baby living there would be bound to grow up happy.

Only . . . their baby didn't look so happy, as Kirsten gently unwound the swaddled blankets and snuggled him down into his fluffy new crib.

As a matter of fact, he didn't look like their baby at all!

"Do you remember him having all this hair?" Kirsten asked, staring puzzled at the bushy shock of curls that sprouted from the baby's head.

"I don't think so," Sandy answered. "Could he have grown it during the car ride home?"

Kirsten shot him a look out of the corner of her eye. "No. He couldn't have."

"Well, he might have," Sandy mumbled, sticking his finger out for the tiny fist to capture again. "How am I supposed to know what babies can or can't do?"

He lightly nudged the baby's hand with his finger, but the little fingers didn't grab on to it. "Come on, Seth," he said, trying again. "You know how to do this."

He tapped the hand again, and when the baby still didn't grab on, Sandy gently took the baby's hand in his own.

"Huh," he said, gazing at the little plastic wristband. "They spelled his name wrong."

"Oh, no," Kirsten said. "I wanted to keep his baby bracelet as a souvenir. How did she spell it?"

"Seth Cone," Sandy read. "C-O-N-E."

He let the small arm drop back onto the blanket, but when he glanced at Kirsten, she was deathly pale and trembling.

"Honey, what is it?" he asked, worried.

Kirsten was shaking her head, barely able to get the words out. "It says that?" she squeaked. "It says 'Seth Cone'?"

"Yes, but —" Sandy started, but she cut him off.

"We picked his name after the nurse had taken him away!" Kirsten told him, her voice rising. "The nurse wrote 'Baby Boy Cohen' on his bracelet!"

Sandy looked at her, not putting the pieces together. "What are you saying?"

"We took the wrong baby home from the hospital!"

"Oh my god!" Summer gasped, bringing a hand to her mouth. "Tell me you're kidding."

"I wish," Sandy said, and despite his best efforts to look as serious as the occasion would dictate, he couldn't stop himself from starting to laugh.

"That's the worst thing I ever heard," Summer said, shooting a guilty look at Seth as she also began laughing.

"Oh, it was terrible," Sandy said, thumping Seth on the back apologetically. "Kirsten was so upset. We couldn't get that baby back to the hospital fast enough. We get there and the nurse is crying, the other mother is crying, Kirsten's crying. I thought your mother was going to strap you to a LoJack after that, so she'd never lose you again."

"You could get him microchipped," Summer suggested. "My stepmonster did that to her Labradoodle, and when he ran away, we were able to find him like two days later."

"I'm not a dog," Seth protested, insulted. "For all I know, I'm not even really a Cohen."

"Oh, you're a Cohen all right," Sandy reassured him. "How else could the Curse of the Cohen have followed you after that?"

"No birthday could have been as bad as that one," Summer said, horrified.

"Please," Seth said. "That experience merely set the stage for the lifetime of bad birthdays that followed."

"Come on, what about when you turned one? How can a one-year-old have a bad birthday?"

"Well, sure, when I turned *one* . . ." Seth started, then stopped abruptly when he saw Sandy grimace. "Are you kidding me?" he asked, outraged. "What in the world happened when I was one?!"

THE OC

1990

"Honey, don't you think you're going overboard?" Sandy said, letting his eyes travel over the mountains of food, games, presents, and decorations that were heaped on every available surface of their tiny living room.

"Seth's only going to turn one once," Kirsten said. "I want it to be special."

"Yeah, but he's *one*," Sandy said, picking up a piñata that was shaped like a donkey eating a churro and peering inside. "He can barely sit up by himself without toppling over; how do you expect him to swing a stick hard enough to whack this open?"

"We have to have games for the older children," Kirsten said. She took the piñata from him and started filling it with candy from a gigantic grocery bag. "The older guests will have fun breaking this, and Seth will have fun watching the candy rain down on him."

Sandy looked doubtful. "That's another thing," he said. "Why in the world did you invite every single kid from his day care? Does he really need thirty kids running around here to help him celebrate his birthday? And more important, do we?"

"It's important to start socializing him early," Kirsten said. "That way he'll have lots of friends growing up."

"Aw," Summer said, looking over at Seth. "I don't know whether that makes me want to laugh or cry."

"Oh, that my social life was completely jinxed by my mother?" Seth snarked. "What's sad about that?"

"You're not jinxed," Sandy told him. "So you went through a rocky patch for a while when it came to friends. That's no big deal."

"If you can call sixteen years a 'patch,'" Seth interjected.

"Well, it looks like things turned out pretty good for you in the end," Sandy said.

Summer leaned over and rested her head comfortably on Seth's shoulder. "They're about to get a lot worse if you don't let your dad finish telling this story," she teased.

"Fine," Seth said. "I wasn't the one who interrupted him in the first place."

"Go on, Mr. Cohen," Summer said, ignoring Seth. "Tell us how you ruined Seth's birthday by throwing him a fabulous party."

"Oh, the party was great," Sandy said. "I'd never seen anything like it."

"What do you think?" Kirsten asked, standing back and admiring her handiwork.

Their little house had been transformed into an authentic

Mexican bazaar. Red, yellow, and orange streamers covered the walls, and huge bouquets of coordinating roses bloomed on every table and countertop. A mariachi band was set up in a corner, piñatas of every shape and size swung gaily from the ceiling, and waiters circulated with platters of ceviche and tostadas and ahi quesadillas. Everywhere you looked were games for the kids, hidden surprises, and, most important, Sandy noted, a uniformed bartender mixing margaritas for the adults in one corner of the room.

They had dropped Seth at the sitter's house that morning so he'd be out of their hair while they got ready for the party, and Kirsten glanced at her watch as she hung up the phone.

"Okay, Nancy's just leaving her apartment with Seth now. The other guests will be here in an hour, and that means I have just enough time to make myself look presentable before everyone arrives."

"You're already more beautiful than anyone who'll be arriving," Sandy said.

"That's so sweet," Summer interrupted again. "It sounds like you guys had a great party planned. Where's the Cohen Curse?"

"Well," Sandy started, but was cut off by the sound of the front door slamming. Ryan and Marissa tumbled into the room, their arms loaded down with shopping bags.

"Hey, guys," Marissa said when she saw them, "what's going on?"

14

"Mr. Cohen was telling us about Seth when he was little. Did you know they almost named him Melinda?"

Ryan and Marissa cracked up and Seth looked indignant.

"That was going to be my name if I were a girl," he protested, and Ryan grinned.

"Well . . ." he started with an evil glint in his eye.

"Don't even say it," Seth said, holding up a warning hand.

The other kids laughed, Seth joining in reluctantly. "Status quo for my birthday," he said.

Ryan blinked. "It's your birthday? Wait — I've known you for almost three years now. How come I haven't ever known when your birthday was?"

"Because for the last two years, you've let me down. Everyone has. And that's why this year I have a new policy: no expectations and no disappointments."

Ryan rolled his eyes. "How could I let you down if I didn't know it was your birthday?"

"Because I'm so used to being let down, I don't even bring it up in the first place."

"Well, that makes sense," Marissa said.

"Yeah," Summer added. "Seth said that every birthday he's had has been bad, but Mr. Cohen's just been telling us about an amazing party they threw for him when he turned one."

"Just because they had a party doesn't mean it was a good birthday," Seth said, and Sandy shook his head.

"I'm afraid he's right."

"Don't tell me no one showed up," Marissa said. "That would be too tragic!"

"Yeah, at least when you're one you don't know any better," Seth said. "Try having no one show up when you're sixteen."

"Oh, everybody showed up," Sandy said. "Everybody . . . except Seth."

The party had been in full swing for nearly an hour and it was hands down a smash success. Everyone was having a great time, except for Kirsten, who was frantically calling the sitter's house every five minutes, wondering where the birthday boy was.

Because the one place Seth wasn't was his birthday party.

"What if something happened?" Kirsten said. "We should call the police."

"I'm sure they're fine," Sandy told her, trying to calm his wife down. "If anything had happened, someone would have called us."

"There could have been an accident," Kirsten persisted. "They could be lying dead in a ditch somewhere for all we know!"

"There are no ditches in San Francisco, sweetie," Sandy said. "If anything, they've driven off a bridge and plummeted to their deaths."

Kirsten lunged for the phone and Sandy put a hand on her arm, laughing.

"I was joking," he said. "They're fine."

But Kirsten just glared at him and dialed the police.

"Yes . . . my son and his sitter were supposed to be here an hour ago — they haven't arrived yet. I'm worried something has happened." She listened for a minute, and then a look of relief crossed her face. "Yes, they were coming that way. Thank you." She hung up the phone.

"A semi jackknifed on the Golden Gate Bridge," she told Sandy happily. "Traffic's been tied up all morning. They're probably just stuck in the jam."

"See, I told you there was nothing to worry about," Sandy said. "Now will you relax and enjoy the party?"

"Definitely," Kirsten said, taking a sip of the margarita Sandy handed her. "Unless —"

"What?"

"Is it wrong for us to have a fun time at Seth's party if Seth isn't even here?" she asked guiltily.

"Nah," Sandy told her, grabbing a taquito off a passing tray. "He's only one. He won't know the difference."

"And if he does, by the time he's old enough to talk, he'll have forgotten all about it," Kirsten agreed.

"Which I had, until you so kindly reminded me now." Seth grinned.

"It was a spectacular party, though," Sandy said. "Doesn't that count for something?"

"It helps prove my point," Seth said, looking on the bright side, "that birthdays, for me at least, are just not worth celebrating."

"You know, it's crazy," Ryan said, "but I also spent my first birthday stuck in a traffic jam."

17

"Really?" Seth asked, surprised.

"Yeah, we were on our way home from visiting my father in prison," Ryan deadpanned. "Still, missing your party — that's gotta suck."

THE OC

1991

"Are we done with this little trip down memory lane?" Seth asked, starting to stand up. But Summer grabbed his hand, pulling him back down onto his stool.

"I like hearing about you as a little kid," she said. "It's cute. I just wish there were pictures."

"Oh, there are pictures of his second birthday," Sandy said.

But Seth shook his head wildly. "No, Dad, please, I beg you. Don't humiliate me this way."

Sandy looked at his son with a solemn expression. "I'm sorry. But I can't help myself. Be right back."

He got up from his chair and hurried out of the room. The other kids looked at Seth, who had his head in his hands and was moaning in embarrassment.

"What could be that bad?" Marissa asked. "Is it you in the bathtub or something?"

"It's a thousand times worse," Seth told her.

19

"I dunno," Ryan said. "My mom used to carry around a picture of me as a baby lying naked on a bed with a daisy sticking out of my butt."

The other kids shrieked with laughter.

"What?!" Summer said. "Why would anyone do that to a baby?"

"I think she saw it on *Benny Hill* or something and thought it was funny."

"Well, it's hysterical," Seth said, "but also very, very cruel."

"Poor baby," Marissa said, rubbing his back. "I will give you a million dollars if you let me see a copy of that picture."

"Never," Ryan declared. "But you see, Seth, we've all had bad pictures taken."

"In my fourth-grade class picture, I'm wearing gauchos, a poncho, and I'm picking my nose," Summer admitted.

"My dad has a picture of me wearing one of my mother's bras on my head," Marissa said. "It's totally embarrassing."

"That sounds adorable," Ryan said. "How old were you?"

"Fifteen," Summer guessed.

Marissa laughed and gave her friend a shove. "Shut up. I was not." She looked down at the table. "I was fourteen."

The others howled. "How 'bout I let you see that if you let me see yours?" she asked Ryan.

But he shook his head firmly. "Not a chance."

"What about you, Picky?" she said to Summer. "Will you show us your picture?"

"Yes," Summer said. "I own my past. And so should you." She poked Seth with her elbow. "However embarrassing this picture is, the only way to release its power over you is to let us see it."

"That's not the problem," Seth said. "You've already seen it. Everyone has."

"We should be finished packing in a couple hours," Kirsten said, handing Seth, a diaper bag, and the gigantic stuffed duck whose beak Seth chewed on instead of a pacifier over to her friend Nora Malta.

"Wait a minute — you know Nora Malta?" Marissa asked, her eyes lighting up.

"Who's Nora Malta?" Ryan asked.

"My former babysitter," Seth said. "It is impressive, I know, that someone would be willing to watch both me *and* the duck. . . ."

"Nora Malta is only about the hottest fashion photographer in the business," Marissa told them. "She's shot the covers of practically every magazine worth reading."

"The *Economist*?" Seth asked. "*Atlantic Monthly*?"

Marissa made a face at him. "Every *fashion* magazine worth reading." She turned her attention to Sandy, who was walking into the room, holding a framed picture behind his back so the kids couldn't

21

see it. "Is it true that Nora Malta used to baby-sit Seth?"

"She lived next door to us in Berkeley," Sandy said. "This was right when she was starting out. She hadn't made a name for herself yet, so she'd watch Seth for us sometimes to earn a little extra money."

"I can't believe you guys are moving away," Nora said, shifting Seth to one hip and taking the diaper bag from Kirsten with the other. "How in the world are you going to adjust to Newport Beach of all places? It's so different down there."

"Well, I grew up in the O.C.," Kirsten said, "so I know I'll fit in. Sandy, though . . . Well, rich people need lawyers just as much as poor people do."

"More, usually," Nora said, and the two women laughed. "What about you?" she asked Seth, lifting him up and blowing noisily on his fat little belly. "Are you going to stay my favorite little Berkeley hippie free spirit?"

Seth laughed and dropped the duck. Then immediately started to cry. Nora set him down on the floor so he could grab it, and as soon as its beak was back in his mouth, he stopped crying and toddled off to explore Nora's living room.

"I hope he's not too much trouble," Kirsten said. "He ate two pieces of birthday cake after lunch, and I'm not sure if he's come down off his sugar rush yet."

The women looked over at Seth, who was spinning around in a circle, making himself so dizzy that he toppled over and landed flat on his back, the duck smothering his face. Seth clambered back up to his feet, giggling, and started to spin again.

"I think I can handle it," Nora reassured Kirsten with a smile. "See you this afternoon."

When Kirsten came to collect Seth a few hours later, Nora met her at the door, waving a set of still-wet contact sheets at her.

"Oh my god, you've got to see these," she gushed. "I snapped a roll of pictures of him right after you left, to see if maybe I could find one that would make a nice birthday present, and they came out amazing."

"Wow," Kirsten said, impressed, as she checked out the pictures on the contact sheets. Apparently it had taken the sugar a while to wear off, because the images showed a beautifully photographed path of destruction, with a tiny, messy, Seth-shaped whirlwind in the center. "These are gorgeous, but I feel like I need to pay you double. He looks like he was a handful."

"Are you kidding? It was worth it to get some of these shots. Seth woke up from his nap while I was still in the darkroom, so I couldn't print any of these for you, but I have one favor to ask."

"Sure. Anything," Kirsten said, still mesmerized by the images on the contact sheets.

"I'm shooting a print campaign for the Karen Black Agency, and I was wondering if you might sign a release so I could use one of these pictures for it."

"You want Seth to be in an ad?" Kirsten asked, surprised.

"You were in a magazine ad?" Summer said, incredulous.

23

"You had your picture taken by Nora Malta?!" Marissa echoed, even more flabbergasted.

"You were a child model?" Ryan asked, mimicking the girls' awed tone, then cracking up. "That's so humiliating."

"Are you kidding? Seth was famous!" Sandy told them. "The agency liked the print ad so much they put Seth in the TV commercial. He was bigger than 'Mikey Likes It' and those Oscar Mayer bologna kids put together."

"But what was the ad for?" Summer asked.

"Glimmer Tile bathroom cleaner," Sandy told them.

Summer and Marissa looked at each other, delighted recognition spreading across both of their faces. "No way," Marissa said. "Do you mean to tell me you were the kid who said —"

"No! Please don't say it!" Seth begged. But it was too late.

"'Uh-oh, where'd it go?'" Marissa and Summer crowed together.

Seth moaned and buried his face in his hands again. But Ryan looked confused. "What are you talking about?" he asked.

"You don't remember that commercial?" Sandy said. "It ran for years. You had to have seen it. Everybody in America did."

A gleaming bathroom. Everything in it is white — glistening white counters, claw-foot tub, sparkling floor. A

white Persian cat sits on a pristine white bath mat. In the midst of all this snowy whiteness, the only splash of color is two-year-old Seth, who sits on the toilet wearing a bright tie-dyed T-shirt and nothing else.

He hops off the toilet and runs out of the bathroom, shouting, "Mommy! I did it! I went potty!"

The white cat looks around, then reaches up a paw and flushes the toilet.

A second later, little Seth races back into the room, followed by a proud mother in a white sundress. He peers into the toilet, then looks at his mom in puzzlement. "Uh-oh. Where'd it go?"

Sandy flipped the framed picture he was holding around to reveal a still image of Seth peering down into the bowl, the hem of his T-shirt barely reaching the top of his naked little butt, with a big bottle of Glimmer Tile featured prominently in the foreground.

Ryan laughed so hard at the image that he had to tilt over in his chair, holding his sides, while tears streamed down his face. "You poor bastard," he told Seth, barely able to get the words out.

"Hey, at least I don't have a flower coming out of my butt," Seth shot back.

But Ryan held up his hands in a gesture of surrender, still gasping to get his breath back. "That's okay. You can see that picture if you want. 'Cause it's not even close to as bad as this."

"I had no idea you were such a star," Summer

joked. "Here I thought the time I appeared in the back-to-school fashion show at the mall was a big deal."

"Too bad you didn't know him then," Marissa told her. "Seth could have given you some tips on how to stay relaxed in front of the cameras."

"Yeah, Seth, you're a natural," Ryan said. He took a closer look at the picture. "You look completely calm. There's no clenching there at all."

"Enough!" Seth begged.

"Yeah, you kids mock," Sandy said, "but that commercial is going to pay for Seth's college."

"Man, Sandy and Kirsten put you through all that and didn't even let you keep the money?" Ryan said to Seth. "That's so wrong."

"Everything about this is wrong," Seth said, and stood up, moving toward the door.

"Aw, Seth, don't leave," Summer said, her tone conciliatory. "We were just teasing. We'll stop."

"Yeah, come on, sit back down," Marissa said. "Don't be mad."

"I'm not mad," Seth said. "I just have to go to the bathroom."

The rest of the gang looked at one another — it was too good to resist. "Uh-oh!" they all shouted at once, but Seth was out the door and down the hall before he had to hear the rest.

THE OC

1992

Seth stayed in the bathroom for as long as he could without it looking like he was avoiding rejoining his friends. Or — doing something that would *take* a long time. Which would be just as embarrassing, actually, if not more so.

He honestly wasn't trying to be a jerk when he said he didn't want to celebrate his birthday. Even though everyone was acting like it was funny hearing the stories about the various disasters that had befallen him, to Seth it wasn't so much funny as . . . agonizing. At least the birthdays he could remember. And maybe Ryan had had worse ones, what with his terrible old life in Chino, but just because Ryan's were bad, that didn't make Seth's any less painful.

When he finally couldn't wash his hands one more time or comb his hair again or linger for one more instant, Seth slowly made his way back to the kitchen. He hoped that in his absence the conversation would have moved onto a new topic. Like the plight of the Sudanese refugees. Or the proper usage of *who* and *whom*. Or whether Summer should use a higher SPF moisturizer now that the weather was getting warmer. Anything, really, no matter how tense or boring or dismal, just as long as they weren't discussing his birthday anymore.

But what he discovered when he got to the kitchen was almost enough to make him want to arrange a screening of that terrible tile cleanser commercial.

Somehow, in the five or six minutes he'd been gone, everyone in the kitchen had time-traveled back to the seventies. Kirsten had arrived home, a guitar had magically appeared in Sandy's hands, and the whole group was watching spellbound as he crooned "I'm All Out of Love" to them.

"What is going on in here?" Seth asked, his jaw dropping.

"Hi, honey," Kirsten said. "Your father was showing Ryan and the girls that adorable picture of you peeking into the —"

"I know the one —" Seth interrupted.

Kirsten blinked. "Well, I thought if we were talking about old times, I'd share this picture of your father —" She held a battered photo out to Seth. It was a picture of Sandy wearing a waist-length wig, gigantic bell-bottoms, platform shoes, and the ugliest disco-style shirt Seth had ever seen.

"Oh my god! What were you *thinking*?" he asked his father.

"Hey, I think I look pretty sharp in that picture," Sandy said, offended.

"But why?" Seth asked again. "Why would you ever dress like this?"

"That was the year I toured with Hair Supply," Sandy said. "I was a real cool customer back then."

"Hair Supply?" Seth repeated.

"It was an Air Supply cover band," Summer informed him. "Isn't that a *riot*?"

"If by *riot* you mean 'deeply disturbing fact,'" Seth answered.

"You loved Hair Supply," Kirsten said. "Don't you remember? You used to get up on the stage and shake your moneymaker for the crowd."

"Okay, first of all, never say 'shake your moneymaker' again," Seth told his mother, "and second, what do you mean I used to get onstage? I wasn't alive in the seventies."

"This was in 'ninety-two," Sandy said.

"You walked around dressed like that in the nineties?!"

"Yes, and the crowd loved it. Oh, man, we had a good time. We'd pile into the car and drive out to parks and state fairs — anywhere we could get a gig. And we'd go wild. My 'Lost in Love' would bring the house down."

"Were you in the band, too?" Marissa asked Kirsten.

"No, I was strictly a groupie," she said. "I was in charge of providing snacks, admiring the lead

29

singer" — she winked at Sandy, who grinned back — "and keeping a tight leash on Seth."

"I thought he was rocking out onstage the whole time," Ryan said, throwing a derisive glance in Seth's direction. "Why was it so hard to keep an eye on him?"

"Usually it wasn't," Kirsten said. "In fact, we only ever lost him once —"

"Wait a minute, you *lost* me?" Seth asked, outraged. "You dragged me to some retro-disco freak show and then lost me?"

"Left at the hospital, lost at the Hair Supply show — seems like somebody was trying to tell you something," Summer remarked casually.

"It wasn't that big a deal," Kirsten said.

"Oh my god, what kind of mother are you?" Seth said, mostly joking, but honestly a little bit hurt.

"We found you practically right away," she said soothingly.

"Still, I could only have been, what, three years old?"

"As a matter of fact," Sandy said, the light coming into his eyes, "this happened on your third birthday!"

"You've got to be kidding me," Seth muttered. But Sandy had already launched into the story.

Seth was too young to understand exactly what birthdays were all about — all he knew was that he was already having the best day. He woke up to a pile of presents at the foot of his bed, then had his favorite foods — hot dogs and

Cheetos — for lunch, and now they were busy getting ready to go to the park for a Hair Supply concert.

Seth jumped up and down with glee — there was nothing he loved more than going to see his dad's band play. He loved the way the audience clapped and cheered for Sandy whenever they finished a song, and he dreamed ~~o~~ day being the one crooning into the mic, while the c applauded *him*.

Torrey Pines State Park, where the concert was being held, was an hour's drive from Newport Beach. The whole ride there, Seth sat in his car seat with his dad's wig on his head, drooping down over his eyes, begging his dad to give him his shot.

"Honey, how about you do your special dance?" Kirsten suggested.

"No! I want to sing!" Seth insisted. "Please!"

"Maybe when you're older and you've learned all the words to the songs —" Sandy started, but Seth cut him off.

"I do know the words!"

Kirsten and Sandy exchanged an amused glance. "Is that right?" Sandy asked. "Well, let's hear 'em."

Seth took a deep breath, pushing the wig back off his forehead so he could see. "*Girl, you're every woman in the world to me*," he sang in his little piping voice. "*You're my fantasy, you're my reality . . .*"

Once again Sandy had to break off in the middle of his story to wait for the other kids to stop laughing.

"Don't mock the Supply," he warned them. "You kids are on thin ice here."

"Sorry," Marissa said between giggles. "It's just so funny thinking of Seth singing that song."

"He has a very sweet singing voice," Kirsten said, making them laugh even harder.

"Cohen! Then how come you've never sere-
_d me?" Summer asked him.

Seth grinned and grabbed a tulip out of the arrangement on the side counter. He handed it to Summer, then put his hands over his heart.

"*Laughing myself to sleep, waking up lonely, I needed someone to hold me, oh . . .*"

"I can't believe you still remember the lyrics," Kirsten said.

Sandy lifted his guitar and strummed along as Seth kept singing, dropping to his knees and grabbing Summer's hand. "*Girl, you're every woman in the world to me. You're everything I need. You're everything to me, oh, girl.*"

He finished with a flourish, and everyone clapped and whistled. Seth took a bow, and Summer threw her arms around his neck in an impromptu hug.

"Who knew that such a dorky band could be so romantic?" she said to him.

"Are you kidding? Air Supply is the music of seduction," Sandy told her. "Matter of fact, that song was playing the first time Kirsten and I ever —"

"Dad!"

"— *kissed*," Sandy finished, with a wicked grin.

Seth looked relieved, and Marissa nudged Ryan with her toe. "Where's my serenade?" she asked him.

Ryan raised an eyebrow. "Let's see —" He

pretended to ponder his options. "I could do that 'rabbits, rabbits, rabbits, rabbits' song from when I played Snoopy."

Now it was Marissa's turn to pretend to consider his offer. "Let's save that for when we're alone," she said.

"You really want me to sing it to you?" Ryan asked, unsure if she was joking.

"No, I mean save it for when I'm alone at my house and you're alone here."

Ryan stuck out his tongue at her, and Marissa turned to Sandy. "Quick, before he starts singing, what happened? Did you give Seth a chance at the mic?"

"I couldn't have stopped him if I wanted to."

Singing to the crowd was even more exciting than Seth ever imagined. Sandy made an announcement that it was his birthday, and people were already clapping for him before he even opened his mouth. He sang the entire song perfectly, not forgetting a single word or losing the melody at all, and when it was finished, he was so electrified by the whole experience that he hopped up and down like a pogo stick for the next three songs in a row.

Between the excitement of the morning's presents and his performance in the afternoon, by the time the concert was over, Seth was so worn out that he could barely keep his eyes open. Kirsten had to carry him to the car, and he made a little nest of blankets in the car seat in very back of their station wagon, so he could take a nap on the way home. Sandy was helping break down the instruments onstage,

33

but Kirsten sat in the backseat of the car so she could read Seth a story until he fell asleep.

Finally Seth nodded off. Kirsten saw Sandy headed toward her, struggling to carry his guitar case, amplifier, and the picnic basket that she'd left behind. He accidentally dropped the basket, and Kirsten rushed over to help him pick up the leftover food and supplies. They finally got everything loaded in the car, and, leaving Seth asleep in the back, drove home.

"But I thought you said you lost him?" Summer said.

"Wake up, sweetie," Kirsten said as the station wagon pulled into their driveway. "Time to go inside and have some birthday cake!"

Seth didn't stir, so when Sandy parked, he walked around to the back of the car. "I've got him," he told Kirsten, tossing her the keys so she could unlock the front door. She started into the house, and Sandy opened up the hatchback.

"Come on, big boy," he said, pulling back the mound of blankets that covered his son.

An instant later he was racing into the house, skidding to a halt in front of a startled Kirsten. "Where's Seth?!" he asked frantically.

"You just said you'd get him," she answered, but he shook his head.

"He wasn't in the car."

"What?!" Kirsten pushed past him as she sprinted out to the driveway.

34

"Can't you drive faster?" Kirsten begged, wringing her hands.

"Honey, I'm already double the speed limit," Sandy said, but he pressed down a little more on the gas anyway.

"I don't understand what could have happened," she said. "He was sleeping! Where could he be?"

Sandy didn't have an answer for her. He swerved around the bend at the entrance to the park and skidded to a stop in front of the now-deserted band shell. He and Kirsten both leaped out of the car, shouting Seth's name.

"Mommy!"

Sandy and Kirsten turned to see Seth skipping toward them, a park ranger striding along on his heels.

"I found him in the middle of the band shell, singing into a twig and making patter with an imaginary crowd," the ranger told them, amused.

"The fans love me," Seth piped up.

"Hey, you had to give the people what they wanted," Sandy said.

"As far as we could figure out, you managed to use the ten seconds I was picking up the picnic things to wake up and pull a Houdini," Kirsten explained. "You were impossible after that — we couldn't take you anywhere with a stage or a microphone without you wanting to get up and belt one out."

"It's worse than I thought," Seth said disbelievingly. "I knew the Curse of the Cohen struck all the birthdays I remember, but I had no idea that it stretched back my entire life."

35

"But that sounded like a good birthday," Marissa said.

"I was abandoned in the woods!" Seth joked. "Happy birthday to me!"

"Hey, at least they bothered to turn the car around and find you," Ryan told him.

"You should be glad we left you there," Kirsten said, "because that was the day you got a new best friend."

Seth thought about this for a minute, then shrugged, baffled. "Sorry, Mom, but I don't remember having any playdates with Park Ranger Pete after that."

"His name was Park Ranger Steven," Kirsten said, "and don't you remember what he gave you when he found out it was your birthday?"

All at once, realization dawned on Seth's face. "Oh my god, he gave me Captain Oats! I'd forgotten all about this. But now I remember it so clearly. He said if I ever got left behind again, I could just ride Captain Oats home."

"Um . . ." Ryan cleared his throat. "Ranger Steven did realize that Captain Oats is plastic, right? And, like, six inches high. And . . . not a real horse?"

"*Shhh*. He'll hear you," Seth hissed. "Captain Oats has very sensitive ears."

"Okay, I guess Seth doesn't realize that either," Ryan murmured to Marissa.

"You really remember all that? Even though you were only three?" Marissa asked skeptically. "I can barely remember things from last week, let alone fourteen years ago."

"Sign of genius," Seth said, tapping the side of his head. "They say Einstein could remember being in the womb."

"Ew!" Summer shuddered.

Seth smiled at his parents. "I take it back," he said. "I guess I did have one good birthday."

"You see?" Sandy said. "A great present can turn the day around."

"I don't know," Kirsten said. "When Seth turned four he got the exact present he asked for, and that was definitely *not* the best birthday he's had."

"Yeah, but it wasn't the present's fault," Sandy said.

"Then whose fault was it?" Summer asked.

THE OC

1993

Seth *knew* there were presents in the house. He could hear them calling to him. It wasn't like Chrismukkah when you had to wait for Santa to bring them to you — Seth knew that the people giving him presents for his birthday were his parents, and he was determined not to wait to start enjoying them.

For weeks now, Seth had been waking up early — even before it was light outside — to start his stealth missions to find his gifts. Sandy and Kirsten never stirred until after *Captain Kangaroo* ended and Bugs Bunny was already two or three cartoons into the show. So Seth would slip out of bed the second he woke up and sneak downstairs, turning on the downstairs TV loud enough so that when he heard the Looney Tunes theme song it was a warning to stop snooping and leave the present search for another day.

The one thing that he was sure of at the end of three weeks of detective work was that the presents weren't hidden anywhere that a three-foot-tall boy could reach. If he wanted to find 'em, he was going to have to go high. It'd be tricky, but all that work would be worth it if the gold at the end of the rainbow was the Hot Wheels Racetrack he'd been dreaming of for months.

Hot Wheels were all the rage in his pre-K class. Timmy Miller had the Deluxe Speedway and eighteen cars, and every day after school Seth would beg his mom to arrange a play-date . . . where he would sit for hours watching in agonizing jealousy as Timmy zoomed the cars around the hairpin turns.

Seth longed to get his hands on one of the cars himself, especially the yellow Corvette with the red racing stripe, but Timmy threatened to beat him up if he so much as touched one of them. No, the only way Seth would experience the thrill of the speedway would be if his parents had taken the hint and bought him a racetrack of his very own.

His birthday was drawing closer and Seth was getting frantic. It was more than just wanting to get his presents early — if he found his cache and the Hot Wheels Racetrack wasn't there, he would need time to mount a full-on campaign of begging and pleading to make sure that Timmy wouldn't be the only one pulling a Mario Andretti every day after school.

On the other hand, he had to be careful. Kirsten had a low tolerance for whining, and he didn't want to run the risk of overplaying his hand. If he begged too much, his parents might get so fed up with hearing about Hot Wheels that he'd blow his shot of ever getting them. So it was imperative that he find them . . . and NOW.

"He couldn't tie his shoes, but if there was a toy he wanted, he would plan such an elaborate strategy that it would make a military advisor's head spin," Sandy said.

"He was like our own little General Schwarzkopf," Kirsten added fondly.

But getting time alone in the house was easier said than done. While Seth considered himself a very mature almost-four-year-old, his mother still seemed to believe that he needed near-constant supervision. So he'd have to limit his treasure hunting to the brief opportunities when his mom was in the shower, on the phone, or otherwise preoccupied.

After his weeks of surveillance, Seth had pretty much narrowed the hiding possibilities down to his parents' bedroom. And a morning spent casing the joint had led him to determine that the most likely locale was his dad's top dresser drawer.

From Seth's vantage point, the drawer was impossibly out of reach. Even with his arms stretched up and standing on tiptoe, his fingers barely brushed the bottom of the drawer, let alone reached the handles. But Seth was determined to find a way in.

The night before his birthday, he finally saw his chance. Jimmy and Julie Cooper had come to have a cup of coffee with his mom, and he could tell from the sound of the laughter pouring out of the kitchen that, as long as he stayed quiet, his mom would assume that he was still parked in the family room in front of *The Wizard of Oz* with Marissa.

If he was going to get into that drawer, it was gonna happen now.

He snuck into his parents' room, the boxes for every board game he owned tucked under his arms. He piled them on the floor in front of the dresser, one on top of the next.

Monopoly, Scrabble, Clue, Mousetrap, all making a staircase that would take him to the Promised Land. He climbed up on top of the Game of Life and, holding his breath, slid open the drawer.

Bingo!

There it was. The Hot Wheels Thunderbolt Racetrack and a box of twenty — twenty! — cars. Seth gasped and nearly toppled off his makeshift ladder in his surprise and delight. This was so much better than anything Timmy Miller had ever even *dreamed* of.

With shaking hands, Seth opened the box of cars and pulled out the little yellow Corvette. He vroomed it along the top of the dresser, and then something else caught his eye. A *second* box of racers. But these were mini. All perfect but only an inch long. Oh my god. It was too much joy for one boy to take!

From downstairs he could hear faint strains of "Follow the Yellow Brick Road" and knew he needed to hurry. He placed the yellow Corvette back in its box, but unable to resist, nabbed three of the little minis. With the box top shut, you couldn't see that they were missing from their plastic compartments. And he just couldn't wait until tomorrow to start having fun.

Shoving the board games haphazardly under his parents' bed, he trundled back down to the living room, where Marissa was devouring a bowl of ice cream and singing along with Dorothy.

"So that was how you grew seven inches that year?" Summer joked, then blanched when the others just stared at her.

41

Seth plopped back on the couch next to Marissa and pulled out his minis. He raced them along the arm of the couch, inventing crashes and chases and spectacular car flips, then stopped when he noticed Marissa staring at him.

"Where'd you get those?" she asked.

"They're a birthday present," he told her, "but don't tell 'cause I'm not supposed to get them till tomorrow."

"I don't have to tell," Marissa said, "'cause here comes your mom, and you're in trouble."

Seth threw a panicked glance at the door. If his mom knew that he'd been snooping, she'd take all the cars away from him for good. He had to hide them — but where?

"Are you guys enjoying your movie?" Kirsten asked, sticking her head in the doorway.

"Yes, Mrs. Cohen," Marissa answered, but Seth could only nod — his mouth was full of mini cars.

"We were going to order a pizza," Kirsten told them. "Pepperoni okay?"

"Sure," Marissa said, then glanced at Seth. "What do you think, Seth?" she asked with a giggle.

Seth stared at her, his eyes widening, then with superhuman effort, he did the only thing he could think of to do. He swallowed.

"Pepperoni's great," he gasped, shooting a triumphant look at Marissa. Kirsten left to make the call and Marissa turned to face Seth.

"I don't think you should have done that," she said, worried. "You're going to be sick."

"Be quiet and watch the movie."

42

"Oh my god," Marissa exclaimed, turning to Seth. "I totally forgot you did that!"

"Yeah, thanks a lot, narc," Seth snarked.

When Seth woke up the next morning, he had an awful stomachache. He didn't tell his mom, though, because he didn't want to ruin his party. But while the other kids were eating the cake and running around, it was all Seth could do to stay upright in his chair.

By the time his parents brought out his presents, any trace of excitement he had over his Hot Wheels track was overshadowed by the terrible, searing pain of the mini wheels racing through his insides. He barely managed to squeak out a halfhearted "Hurray!" when he opened the box.

Sandy leaned over for a closer look at the present.

"What the — there are three missing!" he said. "I'll take these back to the store and get you the complete set."

"Nuh-uh!" Marissa tattled. "Seth ate them!"

Everyone turned to look at Seth.

Seth responded by fainting.

And when he woke up, he was lying in a bed in the recovery room at the hospital, with a three-inch scar on his stomach.

"You told me you got that sailing!" Summer exclaimed, turning on him.

"Sailing . . . car-eating . . . shark-baiting . . . it's all the same, right?" Seth said, and held up his hands to ward her off as she aimed a well-deserved smack at him.

"Shark-baiting?" Sandy looked at his son. "Tell me you don't pretend to have gotten that scar from being bitten by a shark."

"Of course not," Seth reassured him. "At least, not lately."

Sandy laughed and shook his head. "That's my boy."

"At least it sounds cooler than being bitten by a rabbit," Marissa said. "Remember your birthday when you turned five?"

Seth shuddered. "How could I forget? I still wake up screaming sometimes."

Ryan shifted his stool around so he was facing Marissa. "What happened when Seth turned five?"

THE OC

1994

Seth and Marissa carpooled to kindergarten together every day, and every day as they were driving home, Marissa would tell Kirsten or Julie or whomever was driving stories about all the fun things they did and learned that day. She'd recount at length anecdotes about which friends she played with at recess, and whose finger-paintings their teacher, Mrs. Williams, hung up on the wall, and what songs they sang and games they played. Marissa was basically the only source of information about what exactly went on in the kindergarten classroom, because all Seth would talk about was Mitzi, the class guinea pig.

"Ack!" Seth shivered and squirmed as though he were covered in imaginary tarantulas. "I can't even hear that name without completely freaking out!"

"I thought Marissa said you were bitten by a rabbit, not a guinea pig," Ryan said.

"He was." Marissa nodded. "Mitzi was about the most harmless animal you can imagine."

"Wait a minute — I was in your kindergarten

45

class," Summer said to Marissa. "I remember Mrs. Williams, and I remember Mitzi —"

"Stop saying that name!" Seth pleaded again.

"— But I don't remember you being there," she told Seth.

"I always slept on the mat next to you at nap time," he reminded her. "We were class helpers together six times. I gave you the dessert from my lunch every day."

Summer looked doubtful. "Really?"

"We were Tweedle Dee and Tweedle Dum together in the class play."

"I remember being Tweedle Dee. . . ." Summer said, clearly not remembering Seth at all.

"Typical." Seth looked put out. "I went without dessert for an entire *year*."

"You can still sleep next to me at nap time," Summer said, with a flirty smile. But Seth darted his eyes at his parents and made a "shush" gesture with his hands.

"Ix-nay on the ex-talk-say in front of the arents-pay."

They all looked at him with pity. "I can't believe you ever got her to date you, man," Ryan said.

"Can I finish my story?" Marissa asked.

"Please."

All Seth would talk about was Mitzi, the class guinea pig. He was permanently in charge of feeding her and keeping her cage clean, because any time another student wanted

46

a turn, Seth would hover at the poor kid's shoulder, giving such lengthy advice and commentary that eventually no one else in the class would touch the job.

Seth was obsessed with guinea pigs and pets in general. His aunt Hailey had given him a set of the "Olga da Polga" books for Chrismukkah, and he would spend every art period at school drawing comics featuring Mitzi as a guinea pig superhero, who, in a blatant Popeye rip-off, got her strength from eating carrots. He desperately wanted a guinea pig of his own, but a combination of Sandy's allergies and Kirsten's distaste for rodents made the possibility unlikely.

As a special treat for his birthday, however, Mrs. Williams arranged for Seth to be able to bring Mitzi home from school on Friday for the whole weekend.

Seth was ecstatic. He spent Thursday night preparing his room to make it a place where Mitzi could have fun. He made an extensive homemade Habitrail out of cereal boxes and Scotch tape, cleaned the floor so Mitzi could run around, and made sure there weren't any hidden cracks or openings she could squeeze through and run away, then carefully turned the drawer of his nightstand into a temporary cage for her, so he could still pet her even after Sandy had tucked him in bed for the night.

He could barely wait for kindergarten to be over the next day. When it was finally time to go home, he carried Mitzi out to the car, so proud of getting to take her home he thought he'd burst.

He spent the whole evening in his room, watching her run around and play. He even taught Mitzi a wonderful trick, where he'd hold a tiny bit of carrot between his lips and the guinea pig would delicately nibble the other end, so it looked like they were kissing.

"Ew," Summer said. "Cohen, that's completely disgusting."

"I didn't actually *kiss* the guinea pig," Seth said. "It just looked like it. It was a good trick."

"Did Mitzi's mouth actually touch yours?"

"Well, sure."

"Then I don't think mine can ever again." Summer gave a little shudder.

"People kiss their pets all the time," Seth said. "I mean, don't they?"

"*Freaks* do," Summer said.

"When Caitlin had her pony, she used to kiss it on the nose," Marissa said. "It was cute."

"Well, sure, but that's a pony. I kiss Princess Sparkle good-night every night —" Summer said.

"You do?" Marissa said, starting to giggle. "Really?"

"Ha!" Seth clapped his hands. "*Now* who's the freak?"

"Yeah, I would still cast my vote for you, Rat Boy," Summer retorted.

"I don't care," Seth said. "It was still a really good trick."

By the time his parents came in to tell him lights-out, Seth had trained Mitzi so well that whenever he walked into the room, she would come running right over and put her

48

face up to his to look for the carrot, so it really was as if she were kissing him hello. His parents were duly impressed, and Seth fell asleep that night hatching schemes for how he could convince his parents and teacher to let him keep Mitzi forever.

The next morning he awoke to his parents singing "Happy Birthday" to him. After much begging, Kirsten relented enough to let him have Mitzi in her carrier sit next to him at the breakfast table, but nothing could convince her to let him bring the guinea pig to his birthday party, which was being held at the petting zoo in San Diego.

Seth finally decided that seeing all the other animals might make Mitzi jealous, so he agreed to leave her at home while he piled into the car with Marissa and all the other kids from the neighborhood to go to his party.

The party started out well enough. The kids all sang "Happy Birthday," ate cake, and ran around the zoo's playground to work off their excess energy before going into the pen where the petting zoo animals lived. Seth was having a great time, but then he got cocky. He decided to try to teach his kissing trick to the bunnies in the petting zoo. He was sure the other kids would be dazzled and amazed to see the wonderful rapport he had with the animals, like he was Dr. Dolittle or something.

The kids went into the pens, and while Seth's guests were busy petting and playing with the lambs and baby goats, Seth picked out the biggest, coolest bunny he could see — a gigantic black-and-white lop-ear.

"Hey, guys, watch this!" he shouted, glancing around to make sure the other kids were watching, then he slipped between his lips a piece of rabbit chow the zookeeper had passed out. He squatted down close to where the bunny was sitting and puckered up so the rabbit could see the little pellet of food.

The bunny hopped over to him, but instead of daintily nibbling at the morsel, he lunged forward in an attempt to snatch it from Seth's mouth and almost bit Seth's lip!

Seth yelled and yanked his head back, accidentally swallowing the rabbit chow. The bunny, scared by the scream, nipped at Seth again, kicking at his chest with its strong back legs.

By the time Kirsten got to him, the bunny had hopped away, and Seth was in tears.

"Is that why you're so scared of the bunny in *Donnie Darko*?" Summer asked.

"*I'm* scared of the bunny in *Donnie Darko*," Ryan said, "and I've never been to a petting zoo in my life."

"Aw, that's sad," Marissa said. "Never?"

"You poor thing," Summer agreed.

"Hey, I'm the poor thing," Seth said. "I was the one who was terrorized at my own party."

"That seems more *unfortunate* than actually sad," Summer mused.

"You wanna hear sad, listen to how the day ended," Seth told her.

Seth didn't want to go back into the animal pens, so he sat by himself on one end of a teeter-totter in the playground, while the other kids finished playing with the animals.

"You had to teeter-totter by yourself? That *is* sad."

"Shut up."

Finally the party was over, and after they dropped all the neighborhood kids at their houses, they finally made it home. Seth went into the house, wanting nothing more than to lie on his bed and read comics and put the whole day behind him.

But no sooner did he arrange himself on his bed than Mitzi came scampering over, wanting a treat. She scurried up to his face, stuck her little nose out to look for carrots . . . and Seth screamed.

No amount of convincing Seth that Mitzi wouldn't bite calmed him down, and he became so hysterical at Mitzi's continued attempts to do her trick and get her carrot that Sandy finally had to carry Mitzi over to Marissa's house to stay there for the rest of the weekend.

"And I never played with Mitzi again," Seth intoned dramatically.

"I remember," Marissa said. "Finally the rest of us got a turn to be class zookeeper in kindergarten. It was fun."

Seth shot her a betrayed look.

"Well, it was. Before you got all scared and twitchy, no one else ever got to play with Mitzi. I'm sorry, but you getting bitten was the best thing that ever happened for our class."

"I'm glad it worked out for you," Seth said

pitifully. "To this day I can't be around any animal smaller than a cat. That damn bunny still haunts my dreams."

"But it wasn't Mitzi's fault," Marissa said. "It was kind of . . . *your* fault."

"Actually, all of these stories kind of seem like they're your fault," Summer added. "I mean, it sucks that you didn't have a good birthday, but you can't really blame anyone other than your-self."

"I can blame *you* for my next birthday disaster," Seth said, then instantly regretted it. The day he turned six was one of his worst memories, and the last thing he wanted to do was relive the pain of the day, especially with Summer. But it was too late.

"Me?" Summer looked shocked. "What are you talking about?"

THE OC

1995

Today was the day. No more would he stand in the shadows. With one small sprinkled gesture, Summer would finally see him for the man he was. Seth stood outside the door of his first-grade classroom, the box of cupcakes balanced precariously in his hands. He took a deep breath and opened the door.

He walked into the busy classroom and paused, waiting for shouts of "Happy birthday!" And waited. He looked around. Everyone was too busy putting finishing touches on their egg-carton pencil holders to even notice him. He sighed and carried his box to the teacher's desk.

"Ms. Carlson," he whispered to the teacher, "my mom bought cupcakes to celebrate my birthday. Can I pass them out to the class?"

"Not until this afternoon," Ms. Carlson said with a gentle smile and sent him back to his seat.

All day, Seth could barely sit still. He squirmed in anticipation, his eyes riveted to the bakery box that rested untouched at the front of the room. He had gone to the store with his mom, and in addition to the three dozen chocolate cupcakes she had purchased, he had picked out a special one with pink frosting and purple sprinkles, especially for Summer. He knew those were her favorite colors because every day she wore her pink high-tops with the purple laces, and even at six, he knew that the way to Summer's heart was through fashion.

"I remember those shoes," Summer said dreamily. "I loved those shoes. I wore them every day."

"That's what I just said," Seth said.

"This is the best story you've told so far," Summer said, "and I'm not just saying that because it's about me."

After recess, Summer walked by Seth's desk to sharpen her pencil and he suddenly couldn't resist any longer.

"Hey, Summer," he said, breaking into a sweat, "I got cupcakes today."

"So?" Summer said. She tossed her head so her ponytail flipped back and forth. Seth thought it was the most awesome thing he had ever seen.

"It's my birthday," he told her. "And my mom bought extras, so you can have as many as you want."

"Great," she said, bored, and walked away.

Contact! Seth watched her go, sure he'd scored.

The day lasted a million hours. He didn't think Ms. Carlson would ever tell them it was time to put their books away, but finally she did and called Seth to the front of the room.

Seth wiggled with excitement as the class sang "Happy

Birthday" to him. Ms. Carlson had stuck a candle in one of the cupcakes, and when Seth blew it out, he kept his eyes on Summer as he made his wish.

Ms. Carlson was passing out the rest of the cupcakes, but he took the pink-and-purple cupcake and headed toward Summer's desk.

"I brought this special for you," he said, carefully setting the cupcake down on Summer's desk. Summer regarded it doubtfully.

"Did you touch it?" she asked, her nose wrinkling.

"Only on the paper," Seth said. He waited, holding his breath, to see if Summer would accept this token of love.

She narrowed her eyes and inspected the cupcake more carefully. "Are those finger marks in the frosting?"

"No."

"Those look like you stuck your fingers in the frosting," Summer said. "I want one from the box."

"But those don't have purple sprinkles," Seth said, feeling the moment slipping away.

Summer reconsidered. "Fine. I'll have this one," she said. She carefully wiped off the offending finger marks with her finger, wiping the tainted frosting onto a napkin, then peeled the paper away from one edge of the cupcake and took a giant bite.

Seth seized the opportunity. He slid into the desk next to hers and pulled out the present Ms. Carlson had given him — the same book of Mad Libs she gave every student on their birthdays.

"Wanna do Mad Libs with me?" he asked, and Summer shrugged. Seth took this as a yes and opened the book.

"You were a smooth operator," Ryan told Seth. "That was like you guys' first date."

"God, I don't remember any of this," Summer said.

"Good," Seth said. "Then can we just drop it?"

"No, I want to hear the end," Summer said.

Seth blew out a frustrated breath. This story was exactly the reason why he hadn't wanted to let Summer know it was his birthday in the first place. Bad enough he spent his entire school life being a complete outcast until Ryan came. The last thing in the world he wanted was to let the others know just how lonely and humiliated he had been.

Summer had thought he was a loser when they were younger. What if hearing this story made her remember those feelings? Would she think he was a loser again?

"Cohen!" Summer commanded. "Finish the story!"

"Fine. You want to hear what happened?" he said angrily. "You asked for it."

Seth was having the time of his life. While Summer didn't exactly seem to be blown away by the hilarity of his Mad Lib answers, at least she was still playing them with him. And when Seth offered her a second cupcake from the extras left over, she even smiled at him!

Seth also had a second cupcake, then a third and a fourth. He was starting to get a stomachache from eating so many, but he had a feeling that as soon as the party was over, so to speak, he'd have to go back to his own seat, and who knew when he'd ever get Summer to pay this much attention to him again.

So even though his whole body told him not to, he selected a fifth cupcake from the box and made a big show of how much he was looking forward to it.

But the instant he took the first bite, he realized he'd made a terrible mistake. His stomach rebelled, and he was pretty sure if he didn't spit the bite out, his belly would explode. But — there was no way he was going to spit it out in front of Summer. That would gross her out for sure, and then all the progress he'd made with her would be lost.

He'd just swallow this bite, he told himself, and then throw the rest of the cupcake away. So with a giant gulp, he forced the bite down.

"Uh-oh," Ryan said. "I can see where this is going."

For a second, he thought he was going to be all right. But in the next moment, it was all coming back up — that bite, the four previous cupcakes, the peanut butter sandwich and carton of milk he'd had at lunchtime — everything he'd put into his stomach that day came heaving out in a big gush of vomit.

Summer shrieked and leaped away from her desk, and Seth managed to turn his head so he threw up mostly on the floor, making sure none got on her.

Ms. Carlson came running over and sent Seth to the nurse's office while she cleaned up the mess. The nurse checked Seth over, but when he told her how much he'd eaten, she told him there was nothing wrong with him and sent him back to his classroom.

Seth trudged down the hall with a heavy heart. Maybe Summer would feel sorry for him for being sick on his birthday, he decided. But he knew he was kidding himself. He was back to square one with her. Little did he suspect, however, just how bad things would be.

He pushed open the door, and the class all looked up at him. No one seemed particularly horrified — he certainly wasn't the first kid to throw up in school, and he had a glimmer of hope that everything would be okay. But then Summer noticed him and shouted, "Look, everybody! It's Seth Blowin' Chunks!" and the class burst into laughter.

"Oh my god, why are you laughing?" Seth demanded furiously. The last thing he expected when he told this story was that he'd get laughed at *again*! But everyone in the kitchen was cracking up.

"Seth Blowin' Chunks?" Sandy repeated. "You've got to admit that's pretty clever."

Seth's mouth dropped open, speechless at their reaction.

"Come on, Seth," Ryan said, "everyone gets their name made fun of when they're in elementary school."

"All the girls in my Brownie troop used to call me 'Bummer,'" Summer said. "It's not that big a deal."

"Not a big deal?!" Seth exploded. "Do you have any idea of what that did to me? We only had two weeks of school left, and no one would sit next to me that whole time in case I puked again."

Summer rolled her eyes. "Sorry I made you spend two weeks getting teased —"

"It wasn't just two weeks! That was the beginning of me being a complete social pariah!" Seth said. "When we went back to school the next fall, no one remembered *why* they didn't want to be near me, but they kept avoiding me all the same. I trace the misery of my entire school career to that exact moment."

Everyone was silent for a moment as they digested this. After his initial burst of anger, Seth was surprised at how *not* upset he was feeling. Somehow, sitting in the kitchen surrounded by his friends, that long-ago day didn't seem quite as important. Maybe that stupid nickname wasn't wholly responsible for his tragic social life. He always thought of it as the day he lost everything, but actually, it was more like the day he lost his confidence with Summer. Which was a totally different thing. He figured he should say as much to Summer, but then was shocked to see the look of distress on her face.

"Hey, Summer, it's okay," he said awkwardly, but she shook her head.

"I can't believe how mean I was to you," she said.

"It's okay," Seth said. "I mean, it was funny. Seth Blowin' Chunks. Besides, maybe people would have hated me anyway, even if you hadn't said that."

"Oh my god!" Summer buried her face in her hands, racked with guilt.

There was an uncomfortable pause as they all looked around awkwardly, avoiding one another's eyes. And then finally Ryan cleared his throat, breaking the silence.

"While we're stopped — did someone mention ordering a pizza?" he asked.

Marissa thought about it, then perked up. "Kirsten did in a story about two hours ago."

"Well, can we get one now?"

Kirsten nodded and reached for the phone. She carried it into the other room to order the pizza, and Summer lifted her head from her hands.

"How can you eat?" she demanded.

Ryan looked puzzled. "Because I'm hungry?"

"How can you be hungry when I just found out I ruined Seth's life!" Summer wailed.

"You didn't ruin my life," Seth told her, slinging a comforting arm around her shoulder. "Just my birthday. And that would have gotten ruined one way or another anyway."

Summer straightened up, a look of determination on her face. "Well, that's it. This year we're having a party."

Seth shook his head emphatically. "No."

"But I want to make it up to you."

"Yeah?" Seth waggled his eyebrows at her lasciviously. "I can think of other ways for you to do that."

Summer grinned, then tilted her head up to give him a quick kiss.

Ryan turned his head away, feigning disgust. "Do you two want to be alone?" he asked.

Sandy looked up. "No," he said, so pointedly that everyone laughed. "Besides, you're overreacting. Your next birthday was a hit."

"Are you kidding?" Seth asked his father. "It came inches away from ending in tragedy!"

THE OC
1996

It was the most successful party Seth had ever had. He and seven guests went to Legoland, and the afternoon miraculously passed with no one crying, fighting, or getting sick. The kids went on every ride and stuffed themselves with hot dogs and ice cream and generally had a great time.

It wasn't until they had piled, exhausted, into the car to head home that the problems started. Kirsten was doing a head count to make sure they hadn't left anyone behind, when all of a sudden, Seth burst into tears.

"Honey, what's the matter?"

"He's gone!" Seth sobbed.

Kirsten did a second quick count — all the kids were safely buckled in. "Who's gone?" she asked.

"C-C-Captain Oats!" Seth choked out.

Seth had wanted his little horse to share in the fun of the amusement park, so he had snuck him into his backpack and only took him out when Kirsten and Sandy weren't watching. But as they were about to drive away, he realized that he hadn't seen him since they had lunch in the snack bar, three hours earlier.

While Kirsten waited with the other kids at the car, Sandy took Seth back to the snack bar to look for Captain Oats, but he was nowhere to be seen.

Sandy told Seth that he had probably been adopted by some great new family who had a farm where he could run and play, but Seth was having none of it. He threw a tantrum, refusing to leave Captain Oats behind.

"Much like the way I myself had been left behind when I got Captain Oats," Seth reminded his parents.

Sandy and Kirsten rolled their eyes.

Sandy finally talked to the head of maintenance, who led them to the Dumpster where, if he hadn't been adopted by some other kid, Captain Oats would have ended up.

After searching through dozens of drippy, smelly garbage bags, they finally unearthed Captain Oats and Seth was reunited with his friend. Captain Oats was fine — but Seth was covered with so much filth that he ended that birthday in the bathtub.

"Wait a minute — that's what you remember as going bad on that birthday?" Kirsten asked. She, Sandy, and Marissa were staring at Seth in astonishment.

"Of course," Seth said. "I nearly lost Captain Oats! What greater tragedy could there be?"

"Oh my god! How self-absorbed are you?" Marissa asked him.

"I . . . don't know," Seth said, nonplussed. "Why? What else happened?"

"Oh, only Marty Swanson almost dying and your mom having to save him."

"What?" Now it was Seth's turn to gape.

"Hello," Marissa said, "he only went into anaphylactic shock from eating tree nuts —"

"Peanuts?"

"No, tree nuts."

Seth looked at her blankly. "I don't know what you're saying."

"Tree nuts. Nuts that grow on trees. Walnuts, pecans," she explained. "That sort of thing."

Kirsten took over the story. "He was allergic to tree nuts, and apparently the chocolate milk shake he drank while we were waiting for you to dig your horse out of the trash had some nut residue in it, because the next thing we knew, he was lying on the ground twitching and his throat was closing up."

Seth couldn't believe it. "Are you kidding? This happened at my party?"

"Didn't you notice when he wasn't in the car on the way home?" Marissa asked. "And how everyone was talking about him being carted away in the ambulance?"

Seth looked down at the countertop, embarrassed. "I was busy making sure Captain Oats was feeling okay after his ordeal."

"So what happened to Marty?" Ryan asked.

"His mom had given me a syringe of medicine to carry along just in case, so I gave him the shot."

"That's so cool!" Summer said. "Were you scared?"

"I was terrified," Kirsten admitted. "When his mom handed me that syringe when we picked him up, I almost made him get out of the car and stay home. I hate needles."

"Me, too," Sandy told them. "I once fainted at a Berkeley student blood drive."

"You did?" Seth asked, happy the attention was off him for a minute.

"The nurse hadn't even stuck me yet, and I was out cold."

"I've only ever fainted once," Ryan told them. "It was about a year before I came to live with you guys. I was in detention and — you know how you can make a football out of notebook paper?"

"I've seen other guys make them," Seth said sheepishly, "but mine always come unfolded."

Ryan chose to keep his comments about that to himself. "Well," he continued, "I had detention, and this total douche bag Vic Garcia, who was sitting behind me, kept flicking footballs at my back. So finally I turned around to tell him to cut it out, and one hit me in the eye."

"Oh my god! Were you okay?" Marissa asked.

"Well, I went down to the nurse's office, and she drove me to an optometrist."

"Ooh, I hate the eye doctor," Summer said with

a shiver. "The thought of someone touching my eyeball is enough to make me want to faint."

"Tell me about it," Ryan said, wincing at the memory. "This doctor's peering into my eye with his little instrument thingy, and I'm freaking out, right, cause my eye is killing me, and I can't see anything out of it, and there's all this — stuff, this liquid dripping out of the corner of it."

Everyone listening to the story was cringing and had their fingers covering their eyes, as if it were happening to them.

Ryan kept going. "So I'm thinking my eye's been completely poked out, like I'm going to have to get a glass eyeball or something, and the doctor keeps shaking his head and going, 'Oh, dear.'"

"Oh, dear," Kirsten said, not even realizing she was making a joke.

"So at this point I start to hyperventilate, waiting for the news. Finally, the guy picks up this little plastic model of an eyeball, and he takes his pen and he goes, 'If that paper missile had hit you even a millimeter to the left, *this* is what would have happened to your eye. . . .'"

Ryan paused, making sure he had their attention, then continued, using his hands to mime an imaginary pen and model eye. ". . . And he jammed the pen into the plastic eyeball and ripped it open!"

They all squealed.

"So what happened?"

"I fainted and fell out of the chair!" Ryan said with a laugh. "I woke up five minutes later flat on my back on the floor."

"Was your eye okay?" Marissa asked.

"Yeah. I had to wear a patch for a few weeks, though — it made me look like a complete tool."

The doorbell rang, and Sandy jumped up. "Pizza's here!"

"God, who could eat after a story like that?" Summer asked.

Without missing a beat, everyone in the kitchen held up a hand.

"Me too," Summer admitted, and Sandy left to get the door.

THE OC
1997

Five minutes later, they were all biting into the thick cheesy slices.

"You know, I don't think you can count Legoland as being cursed," Marissa said through a mouthful of pepperoni. "Because the party was technically over by the time Marty went into shock — and Captain Oats got out of the barn. And up until then, that party was a blast."

"Hey, Coop," Summer said, "how come you were at all of Cohen's birthday parties?"

"I lived next door to Seth practically my whole life," Marissa said. "Every kid on this street went to his parties."

"But he never came to any of your birthdays," Summer said.

Marissa looked guilty. "That's 'cause I had friends."

"Hey, I had friends too," Seth said, offended.

There was a silence, where no one would meet his eyes. Including his parents.

"You did?" Summer finally asked, trying hard not to sound too incredulous.

"Yes," Seth insisted. "Carl Triola. In third grade. We were *best* friends."

"Who?" Marissa asked.

"Carl Triola. He was in our class. Short kid, big glasses, always reading X-Men comics," Seth elaborated.

"Oh, wait —" Summer said, thinking hard. "Was he that little dweeby kid who set off the alarms when we had that field trip to the natural history museum, because he wanted to pet the dinosaurs?"

"No, that was me, " Seth said with a sigh. "Carl Triola was the coolest kid in the entire school."

Carl Triola was so cool. Seth watched him struggling with the armload of comics weighing him down, his bottle-bottom glasses glinting in the sunlight. And when Carl looked up and smiled a wide, gap-toothed grin, Seth knew instantly that they were destined to be friends.

They had everything in common — they both preferred Marvel to DC, *Dr. Who* to *Star Trek,* Super Mario Brothers to Lara Croft. Seth had never had a real best friend before, and he couldn't believe what he'd been missing.

Within days of finding each other, Seth and Carl were inseparable. They sat together in class at school, passing notes written in the secret code they made up, and every afternoon would go to Carl's house to work on the robot they were building. Carl slept over at the Cohens' practically every weekend, and they would spend hours looking through Sandy's old telescope, ostensibly to identify constellations, but really in the vain hope of spotting a UFO.

"Okay, I remember him now," Summer said. "He used to get nosebleeds whenever the teacher called on him."

"That was me again," Seth said wearily.

So when Seth's birthday was approaching, the two boys could talk of nothing else. For weeks they debated what kind of party Seth should have. Would it be weird to build a haunted house in May? Could they convince Seth's parents to hire a juggler? Should they practice a magic act they could perform for the guests?

After changing their minds a thousand times, they finally came up with a perfect theme: pirates! Seth would dress up as Long John Silver and Carl would be Captain Hook. They planned out a hunt for buried treasure, Seth begged Kirsten to rent a parrot to add an air of authenticity to the occasion, Carl learned how to play "Sixteen Men on a Dead Man's Chest" on his harmonica, and they included an eye patch with each invitation, so the guests would look like pirates, too.

"You totally could have come," Seth told Ryan, "since you'd poked your eye out with that paper football."

"If only I'd known," Ryan agreed, in as sincere a voice as he could manage.

Seth was already over the moon with excitement, and then the day before his party, Sandy came home with news so good Seth thought he was going to burst with happiness: One of the lawyers he worked with owned a schooner that he was willing to lend to the Cohens for the party! After games and cake at the Cohens' house, Sandy would drive the kids down to the marina, where Seth could run a skull-and-crossbones up the mast, and they could cap off their pirate party with a ride on a pirate ship!

Seth couldn't believe it. Sailing was already one of his absolute favorite things in the world to do. He took sailing lessons every summer at day camp and was already saving his allowance and Chrismukkah money so he could buy a sailboat of his own. He and Sandy had been fixing up an old boat that Sandy bought the previous summer, but it wasn't seaworthy yet. Seth could hardly wait until their boat was in good enough shape to take out, but in the meantime, this boat ride would be the crowning touch to an already splendid occasion.

Seth hugged Sandy hard, shouting, "Thank you!" and "Yippee!" and "Avast, ye mateys!" Then he ran to the phone to call Carl with the amazing news.

Seth blurted out the information about the boat ride, talking so fast that Carl could barely get a word in edgewise. When he finally stopped for a second to catch his breath, all Carl said was that his mother was calling him for dinner, and he had to hang up.

Seth put the phone receiver back on its hook and ran back into the living room to hug his dad again.

The next morning, Seth was up at the crack of dawn.

The party started at noon, and Carl was supposed to come over early to help him set up the treasure hunt and get into their pirate costumes, but Seth couldn't wait to get started.

He and Carl had painted an old shoe box to look like a treasure chest, and he filled it with the Hanukkah gelt that Kirsten had driven around half of California to find. When he was finished, it really looked like pirate booty, and Seth reverentially carried it down to the hiding place they had selected and marked on a treasure map.

By the time he finished planting all the clues that would lead the party guests to where the chest was buried, it was after eleven. Kirsten was already back from the bakery where she had ordered an anchor-shaped cake and was busy blowing up balloons and filling goody bags with toy boats, *Treasure Island* comic books, and more of the gelt.

"You better go get your outfit on," she told Seth when he came wandering into the house.

"Carl isn't here yet," Seth informed her.

"I'm sure he's on his way," Kirsten said. "If he doesn't get here by noon, we'll call him, okay?"

"'Kay." Seth ran upstairs to his room and started changing into the pirate costume he'd assembled. He was wearing black pants that he'd Scotch-taped a bunch of gold braid to the outside of the legs and one of Kirsten's puffy silk blouses as a shirt. He'd made a sword out of cardboard and slung that through one of Sandy's black leather belts, and when he'd opened his presents that morning, he'd been delighted to find an authentic pirate hat among them. His parents had refused to rent a real parrot for him, but

Kirsten had found an old stuffed one in a thrift store, and he affixed that to his shoulder. He put everything on and went to admire himself in his parents' full-length mirror.

He looked fantastic, if he did say so himself. He couldn't wait for Carl to see him, whenever he finally got there. Where the heck was he anyway? Then he heard his mom calling from downstairs.

"Seth! Your guests are arriving!" she said, and Seth thundered down the stairs, hoping it was his best friend, but finding instead Marissa, in a pink dress and the eye patch.

"You wore the eye patch?" Ryan said, surprised.

"'Course," she answered breezily. "Even at eight, I knew how to accessorize."

More guests arrived in the next few minutes, but there was still no sign of Carl. Seth was going crazy, bugging his mom to call Carl's parents and see where they were, when the phone rang.

Seth grabbed it before it finished even ringing once. "Where are you?" he demanded into the phone, in lieu of hello.

"Happy birthday, Seth." It was Carl's mom. "Can I speak to your mother, please?" she said.

Seth handed the phone to Kirsten, who listened for a few moments without saying anything.

"Where is he?" Seth asked again, tugging on his mom's sleeve.

"Carl doesn't have to ride on the boat," Kirsten finally

said into the phone. "He can come for the party at our house, then stay on the dock while the other guests go sailing." She listened for a minute. "I understand, but it's so important to Seth. . . ."

Seth watched, holding his breath. He couldn't have the party without Carl there — it wouldn't be any fun without him.

Kirsten finally bent back down to Seth and gave him a little hug. "Carl's not coming, honey," she told him. "He wants to talk to you, though."

She handed the phone to Seth, who brought it to his ear, horrified to feel his eyes starting to fill with tears. "Where are you?"

"I don't want to go on the boat," Carl said. "We never decided we'd have a boat."

"But why can't you come for the treasure hunt?" Seth asked.

"Because everyone'll make me try to come sailing," Carl said. "Even if now they say they won't, when it's time to go to the marina, they'll try to convince me that I'll have fun, and I don't want to go!"

Seth could hear Carl starting to cry, and it made him even more upset. "Then we'll just cancel the boat ride," he said. "We'll tell them no one can go."

"No," Carl said. "'Cause then everyone will hate me for ruining the party."

"I hate you!" Seth shouted. He dropped the phone and ran out of the kitchen, crying openly now. Behind him, he could hear Kirsten talking to Carl's mother, and he knew the other party guests were staring at him, but he didn't

74

care. He fled to his room and threw himself down on the bed, sobbing into his pillow.

After a few minutes, Kirsten came in. She convinced him to come down and join the party, but all the activities he and Carl had so carefully planned held no pleasure for him now.

"That's so sad," Summer said, looking like she was going to cry herself.

"I was so mad at that kid," Sandy said. "Even though it's not his fault he was afraid, I still wanted to go over there and drag him to the party."

"Whatever happened to him?" Marissa asked.

"He came over the next day and said he was sorry," Seth said. "He gave me a Game Boy as a birthday present, so I forgave him, but his family ended up moving away that summer anyway."

"Cohen's right — his birthdays suck," Summer said. "These are the most heartbreaking stories I've ever heard."

"I got a Game Boy for my birthday once," Ryan said, keeping a very straight face. "Trey had stolen it from a Radio Shack. Then he sold it to buy drugs."

Summer looked at him for a long minute, then shrugged. "But that was Chino," she said. "These are the saddest *Newport* stories."

"If you feel that bad for me, maybe you could let me have that last piece of pizza?" Seth asked in a pitiful little voice.

Summer looked down at the slice in her hand, then handed it over to him. "Okay, but if your next birthday only sucked because you got chocolate cake instead of vanilla, or something lame like that, you're buying me a whole pizza of my own."

"No, his next birthday was pretty bad," Kirsten said, "but this one was all my fault."

1998

The debate about whether or not to get Seth a skateboard for his birthday had been going on for weeks.

Kirsten thought they were too dangerous. Seth was not exactly the most coordinated boy around. Knowing him, he would fall off it and break his neck, or lose control, roll into the street, and be hit by a truck.

"Gosh, Mom, thanks for the vote of confidence."

She also thought he was just too little. Nine was pretty young to be risking life and limb at the local skate park. Besides, Seth was so scrawny and pale, he looked a lot younger — and more delicate — than he actually was.

"Gee, it just keeps getting better and better," Seth remarked wryly. "Did my chronic bed-wetting also factor into the decision?"

Summer opened her mouth, and Seth held up a finger to silence her. "Joking. I stopped wetting the bed *months* earlier."

Sandy, on the other hand, was all for getting it for him. If Seth learned how to skateboard, maybe that'd give him the balance and confidence to come surfing with him sometime. Sandy was *dying* to teach Seth how to surf. Besides, Seth had such an avid hatred of all things athletic that Sandy believed they should encourage any hint of desire to try something physical.

And if there was one thing Seth had, it was desire. He read and talked about skateboarding all the time. Although he'd never actually set foot on a real skateboard, he was pretty sure that his experience reading about it would translate.

Still, he went to bed the night before his birthday unsure if there would be a skateboard in the pile of presents at the foot of his bed when he woke up the next day.

But when he opened his eyes the next morning — score! Not only had they gotten him the exact model he wanted but Aunt Hailey's present to him was a packet of Ninja Turtle decals he could use to customize it.

"Ninja Turtles?" Marissa asked, starting to laugh.

"I was nine," Seth said. "Ninja Turtles are still cool when you're nine, right, Ryan?"

"Definitely." Ryan nodded. "I had a Leonardo Trapper Keeper that I carried around until the fifth grade."

"That's so cute," Marissa said, and Seth held his hands out in annoyed confusion.

"Wait a minute. How come when I like the Turtles it's geeky, but when Ryan likes them it's" — he raised his voice to mimic Marissa's — "*sooo cute!*"

Summer and Marissa looked at each other and shrugged. "Well, 'cause he's all tough and silent and tortured and you're all . . . Cohen," Summer said.

Seth looked at Ryan, exasperated. "Do you believe this?"

But Ryan wasn't paying attention. "You think I'm silent and tortured?" he asked the girls, who nodded.

"Yes, but in a hot way. Like James Dean."

Ryan grinned, and Seth threw up his hands. "I give up. Go on with the story, Mom."

Seth begged for a chance to try out his new skateboard before school, so Sandy took him down to the beach. Seth took off like a pro, skating smoothly along the path by the edge of the water, barely wobbling at all, and never once faltering or losing his balance, until he got to the edge of the skate park, where a bunch of teenagers were doing flips and tricks on the giant U-shaped ramps.

Seth stared at them, his mouth open in wonder. One day he'd do tricks like that, he decided. He looked down at his skateboard — maybe his dad would let him try it now, to see what it felt like to soar down the giant curves. He skated to the edge of the pipe and started to climb up it.

"Whoa! Whatcha doing there?" Sandy asked, putting a hand on his shoulder to stop him.

"Gonna go catch some air," Seth said in his toughest voice, pointing to the top of the highest ramp.

"That's a little steep," Sandy said, shaking his head, and looked around. "Come on. Let's try this one over here."

He led Seth to a long zigzagging slope. It wasn't even close to being as high, but there were other, older kids whizzing down it, so Seth knew that it wasn't just for babies.

Without pausing, he clambered to the top of the ramp and hauled his skateboard up after him.

"You ready?" Sandy asked. "When I count to three, you push off."

Seth nodded. The ramp looked infinitely long, but he wasn't scared.

"One, two, three!" Sandy shouted, and Seth threw himself down the slope.

His skateboard picked up speed, going so fast that even Sandy running alongside couldn't keep up. Seth was having the time of his life. The wind was whipping through his hair, his ears were filled with the noisy rumble of wheels on wood, and he felt like he was flying. He never wanted to walk again.

He reached the end of the ramp and then realized he had no idea how to stop. He tried putting a foot down off the skateboard to drag along the ground, but all that did was lurch him into a dizzy circle. He spun out, the top of his skateboard jumping over the wooden rim of the slope, and he pitched over into the grass, the skateboard landing on top of him with a thump.

Sandy ran over to him to —

"Wait a minute!" Kirsten said. "You never told me about this."

"I didn't want you to worry," Sandy said soothingly.

"Well, I would have worried," she said angrily. "He was only nine, and you let him rocket down a steep hill? This is exactly why I didn't want him to get a skateboard. He could have shattered his spine and ended up paralyzed."

"But he didn't," Sandy said. "There wasn't a scratch on him."

"See, Mom?" Seth said, holding up his arms and spinning in a slow circle. "No wheelchair."

Kirsten didn't look satisfied. "I knew that skateboard was too much for him. He could really have been hurt." She frowned at Seth.

"Mom! Come on," Seth said. "I laugh at danger. Tony Hawk takes lessons from *me*. I can't get hurt — I'm just that good."

Summer snorted, and Seth glanced at her, wounded. "I *am*. You've never even seen me do my ollie kickflip," he said, and Summer quickly apologized.

"I know, you're right, and thank you for not ever making me go down to that nasty skate park with you when I could be doing, oh, basically any other thing on earth that would be less sweaty and boring."

"I'll forgive you if you admit that I'm the best skateboarder you've ever seen."

"How about I admit you're the best skateboarder I've ever actually spoken to?" Summer bargained.

"Good enough."

"Sounds like you were a pretty cool little kid," Ryan said, impressed.

Seth glowed at the compliment.

"Finish the story, Sandy," Ryan said. "Did you let him get up on the half-pipe after school?"

"I had a court date," Sandy said. "Kirsten was the one who was supposed to take him back to the skate park that afternoon."

Kirsten didn't know what to do. She'd spent the morning working with her father on the plans for a new development that the Newport Group was building. At lunchtime, she drove out to meet with a new contractor at his current construction site, a good hour up the coast near Santa Barbara, while Caleb stayed behind in Newport to finish his business there. If things had gone according to schedule, she would have been back in the O.C. in plenty of time to pick Seth up from school.

Things, of course, didn't. One mini-disaster after the next, culminating in her car breaking down on the highway north of L.A., conspired to make her realize that she'd be lucky to make it home in time for dinner, let alone in time to pick up Seth.

Usually the housekeeper would be happy to fetch Seth if they needed her to, but she had asked for the afternoon off, and Kirsten didn't know how to reach her. Julie Cooper probably wouldn't mind watching Seth for the afternoon, but there was no answer when she tried calling the Cooper household. Kirsten phoned one friend after the next, desperate for someone who would be able to collect Seth and babysit him until she could get home, but no one she tried was available. Sandy was already in court and unreachable, and Kirsten was getting frantic. She had this terrible vision of poor little Seth, waiting alone and abandoned on the bench outside the school, on his birthday, no less! There had to be *somebody* who she could trust with her son.

Finally Kirsten had run out of options. There was only one person left to call, and she had a feeling that Seth might be happier if she just left him on that bench. She took a deep breath, picked up the phone, and called her father.

"What are you doing? Stop that!" Caleb said. He strode over to where Seth was fastidiously putting the Ninja Turtles stickers on his skateboard.

"The original *Pimp My Ride*," Seth said, cracking himself up.

"What's the matter with you?" Caleb demanded. "That's a brand-new toy and you've vandalized it already."

"It's not a toy, it's a deck," Seth said, "and the stickers are *supposed* to go on it. That's what makes it cool."

Seth was probably the only person in Newport Beach who wasn't afraid of Caleb Nichol. He knew his grandfather was essentially harmless, at least as far as Seth was concerned. That didn't stop him from getting yelled at by the old man, but Seth was pretty good at taking it all in stride.

"I suppose next you'll think it's 'cool' to cover yourself in tattoos and play your music so loud you damage your hearing."

"I miss Grandpa," Seth remarked.

"Really?" Sandy asked, surprised, then caught

Kirsten's look. "*Really*," he repeated emphatically, nodding a few times to demonstrate exactly how much he missed Caleb, too.

"I mostly just want to learn how to skate the half-pipe," Seth said, "although a tattoo might be okay, too." He was kidding, but as usual, Caleb completely missed the joke.

"You're getting older now," he lectured, "and it's time you grew up. Started accepting some responsibility."

"Yes, Grandpa."

"You're becoming a man, and it's high time you started acting like it."

"Yes, Grandpa."

"I know your father doesn't hold you to a higher standard, but you're a Nichol, and that's a name that means something."

"Yes, Grandpa."

Caleb gazed sternly at his grandson. "Are you just saying 'yes, Grandpa' because you think it's what I want to hear, or do you actually understand what I'm saying?"

"I understand. You're telling me that with great power comes great responsibility."

"Exactly." Caleb nodded, satisfied, and Seth grinned.

"Can we go to the skate park now, Grandpa? Mom promised me I could for my birthday."

"Certainly," Caleb said. "But first I think we need to talk. You're what now — eleven? Twelve?"

"Nine."

"Well, nine's old enough to hear what I have to say."

"Oh my god, did he give you the sex talk?" Marissa asked, wrinkling her nose. She couldn't have imagined discussing so much as the weather with Caleb, let alone sex, but Seth shook his head.

"No. He talked to me about annuities and asset allocation funds." Seth paused to let the sheer boredom of what he'd just said sink in, then delivered the kicker. "For *four hours.* By the time he finished yammering on about maximizing my 401(k), it was dark out, and we had to skip the skate park."

"I felt so guilty about abandoning you on your birthday," Kirsten said. "That's the only reason I ever let you try that half-pipe, you know."

"Really?" Seth brightened. "I guess that wasn't such a bad birthday after all, then."

"And I believe *I* was the one to give you the sex talk," Sandy said, "and correct me if I'm wrong, but I gave it to you exactly one year later, on your tenth birthday."

Seth blushed, and Summer grinned. "Wow, that's some pretty advanced stuff for a ten-year-old. My dad *still* thinks I'm too young to hear about it."

"Well, I wasn't planning on giving Seth the Talk quite that early," Sandy said, "but he forced my hand."

"Really?" Ryan perked up. Now they were getting to the good stuff. "What'd he do?"

THE OC
1999

"My tenth birthday had so much promise," Seth said wistfully. "It seemed like fate that the most monumental occurrence of our childhoods happened on my birthday."

"What are you talking about?" Summer asked.

"May sixteenth, 1999," Seth said significantly.

The others looked at him blankly.

Seth blinked, shocked. "Are you telling me you don't remember what happened on that day?"

"Why don't you tell us?" Ryan suggested.

Seth opened his eyes wide, his whole body quivering with the significance of the event. "May sixteenth was opening day of *Star Wars: The Phantom Menace!*"

The other kids groaned. "*Star Wars*?" Summer echoed, her voice dripping with disdain. "Please. The old *Star Wars* was okay, just because Luke was cute —"

"You liked Luke?" Marissa asked, turning to face Summer with interest. "I thought Harrison Ford was so much hotter."

"Yeah, but I can't see him without picturing him the way he looks today. He's so — craggy."

"Is he still dating Ally McBeal?" Marissa wondered. "I always thought they were such a weird couple."

"*Ally McBeal* sucked," Summer said. "Why were they always singing? And unisex bathrooms are just gross."

"Excuse me," Seth said, annoyed, "but I believe we were talking about *Star Wars*."

"That's why we changed the subject," Summer told him.

"Really, man," Ryan added, "*Phantom Menace* sucked."

"True," Seth conceded, "but it sucked for a *Star Wars* movie, which still puts it ahead of practically every other movie out there."

"Agree with you, I don't," Marissa said in a Yoda voice, and the other kids looked at her like she was insane.

"What are you talking about, Coop?" Summer asked, baffled.

"I was doing Yoda."

"Well, don't."

"I liked your Yoda," Seth said. "And I also liked *Phantom Menace*. I mean, I wouldn't watch it again. . . ."

"Then why did you make me buy you the DVD?" Sandy asked, amused.

"I had to have the complete set," Seth said. "Besides, I still think it's cool that it came out

87

on my birthday. I only wish I could have seen it then. . . ."

Seth was arguably the biggest *Star Wars* fan in Southern California. He'd never forget the first time he saw it. They were doing a revival of all three movies at the Paradise Theater in Newport, and Sandy had taken Seth to see the first *Star Wars* movie one evening while Kirsten was working late.

Seth had sat spellbound throughout the movie, so riveted to the screen that he barely blinked. He was completely absorbed by the story and the possibility of such adventure. The first movie ended, and Seth refused to leave the theater. Even though it was already getting close to his bedtime, he convinced Sandy to stay for *The Empire Strikes Back*. If anything, that one entranced him even more. And although it really was too late for them to stay and watch the third movie that evening, the next night he wheedled Sandy into going back and completing the trilogy.

Since then, he'd watched all three movies so many times that he could quote every line along with it. He referred to the family car as the *Millennium Falcon*. He'd spent weeks drawing a comic about the adventures of Boba Fett. He'd dressed up as one character after another from the movie every Halloween since he could remember, including one regrettable year when he thought it'd be funny to go as Princess Leia. And he owned two complete sets of action figures — one to play with and one kept pristine in its original packaging, which he was sure would be worth enough one day that he would never have to work again — not that he'd ever consider selling it, of course.

So when he learned that the newest movie was going to be released on his birthday, he took it as a sign from the Force. Seth was secretly convinced that this meant that he was, in fact, the last of the Jedi Knights, who had been hidden with the Cohens for safekeeping until the time was such that he would be called upon to help defeat the Empire.

"After I read Harry Potter I thought the same thing," Marissa said. "I was sure that I would wake up one morning with an owl flying through my window to drop off my invitation to Hogwarts."

"So did I," Seth exclaimed. "I figured my wizarding powers could only help me battle Darth Vader."

"I used to pretend I was part of the cast of *The Valley*," Summer said wistfully. "And Grady would dump April and take me to prom."

"Yeah, not really the same thing," Seth said, not unkindly.

"I never thought anything like that," Ryan said. "Playing air guitar along with my Journey CD was about as close as I got."

"That's because you are very sad and unimaginative," Seth told him, and got back to his story.

Seth told his parents that instead of a birthday party that year, he wanted to go see *The Phantom Menace* with some guys from his sailing class. None of them were as big fans of the franchise as he was, but he needed the company because, as the second, more controversial part of his request, he wanted to see the movie without his parents.

Kirsten and Sandy weren't sure, but Seth had worked his argument out beforehand. He was ten now. That was double digits. Surely that meant that he could be trusted to be dropped off at the multiplex and not get lost, hurt, or kidnapped for the two hours until they came to pick him up again. His parents finally agreed, and Seth was ecstatic.

The day the movie opened, Sandy dropped Seth and his three sailing pals off at the theater, with enough money for tickets and popcorn, and with the admonishment for the boys to be good and have fun.

As exciting as being out without his parents was, for Seth the real excitement came from seeing the crowd at the theater. Half the people there were wearing costumes — Seth half-wanted to call Sandy back, to take him home to change into one of his Halloween extravaganzas. The air felt electric — Seth hadn't ever met anyone who liked the movies as much as he did, and it was gratifying to see that there were others out there who were as rabid as he.

The four boys got into the back of the ticket line, and after lots of jostling and shoving — mostly of one another, and only a little bit of the people in front of them — finally made their way to the counter.

"Four for *Star Wars Episode One: The Phantom Menace*," Seth said, pulling two of the twenties Sandy had given him carefully out of his pocket and setting them on the counter.

"Which showing?" the bored-looking box office girl asked.

"Uh — this one. Two-fifteen," Seth said.

"It's sold out," the girl told him.

Oh, no! Seth's heart sank. Why didn't they think to buy the tickets beforehand? This was a nightmare.

He leaned back to check the times listed on the marquee. The movie was showing in several theaters; maybe they'd have better luck with another one. "Okay, then four for the three-oh-five, please." They'd have to find a pay phone to let Sandy know to come get them later, but Seth was pretty sure it'd be okay.

"That's also sold out." The girl tapped a couple keys on her computer, then looked up at Seth. "There's one ticket available for the eleven-twenty showing tonight, or else tomorrow we have four seats in the eight A.M. showing."

Seth stared at her, stricken. This was the worst possible thing he could imagine. "But — it's my birthday," he said in a small voice, knowing it wouldn't make a difference, but unable to stop himself.

The girl's expression didn't change. "Is there a different movie you want to see?"

Seth and his friends looked at one another. "How about *Tarzan*?" Lonnie asked. He was a shrimpy little kid who always wore a bright green life jacket when they were sailing — Seth almost hadn't recognized him without it when Sandy picked him up that morning.

"I've seen *Tarzan* about six times already," Pete said. He was the best sailor in their class, and also the bossiest. Seth actually didn't really like him very much. But Pete was the only one of the other kids who seemed even close to being as excited about seeing *Star Wars* as Seth was, so he'd thought it would be okay having him along. Now he wished he hadn't invited him.

"I've seen it, too," Seth said, "but I guess we could watch it again."

"No way," Pete said. "What else is playing?"

"The only other movie showing at this time is *The Mummy*," the bored box office girl told them.

"That's supposed to be awesome," Marc piped up. He was the third kid Seth had invited along, and the one he liked best.

"Okay," Seth said with a shrug. He was bitterly disappointed, but he figured he might as well make the best of things and try to enjoy his birthday anyway. Besides, *The Mummy did* look awesome. "Four for *The Mummy*, please," he said and slid his money to the girl.

The boys loaded up on candy and snacks and walked down the long hall toward the theater where their movie was playing.

"You guys, I have an idea," Pete said. "Let's sneak into an R movie instead."

"I kind of want to see *The Mummy*," Seth said.

"You can see that anytime," Pete told him. "But now's our only chance to see something *good*."

Seth thought that *The Mummy* would be good enough for him. Besides, it had taken enough convincing to get his parents to let him go to the movies alone — he didn't want to do anything to jeopardize them letting him do it again in the future.

"I don't think we should," he said, looking to Marc and Lonnie to back him up. "We could get in trouble."

"Don't be a baby," Pete said. "No one's gonna know."

"I've never seen an R movie," Lonnie said hesitantly. "I wouldn't mind sneaking into one."

Marc gestured to the sign above the theater they were

passing. "I heard this one has a girl's naked boobs in it!" he told them.

"All right!" Pete said, and, glancing around to make sure no grown-ups were watching, pushed the door open and went in.

Lonnie followed him, and Marc paused at the door. "Come on, Seth," he said. "It'll be okay."

Seth hesitated. This was not at all the way he had envisioned spending his birthday. On the other hand, he was kind of curious about what a real live boob looked like.

"Okay," he said, and with a quick glance around, darted inside.

"Wait a minute," Ryan said. "You haven't told us what the movie was."

"Ah," Seth said, "that's because it was so spectacularly inappropriate, I wanted to make sure you all give it the proper attention and gravity it deserves."

He looked around to make sure he had everyone's attention, then with a flourish, announced the title. "We snuck into . . . *Eyes Wide Shut*."

The other kids cracked up.

"I guess you got to see a boob and then some," Marissa said.

Seth sat frozen in his chair, unsure how he was suppose to react to the things they were watching. My god, is that what grown-ups actually *did*? Did his *parents* do things like that? He knew — although he didn't like to think

93

about it — that his parents must have had sex at least once for him to have been born. . . .

"Oh, we've done it more than once," Sandy said with a sly grin.

"Sandy!" Kirsten blushed and gave him a playful slap on the arm.

"Yeah, still don't like to think about it," Seth said, wincing.

. . . But he couldn't imagine — didn't *want* to imagine — them doing the sorts of things the characters onscreen were doing.

At age ten, Seth's entire knowledge of sex came from rumors he'd heard from the other boys at school; the dirty passages in a Robert Heinlein novel Kirsten had bought him, mistakenly thinking it was one of Heinlein's kids' books; a little clandestine experimentation when he was in the shower; and the vague, tingly feelings he got whenever he saw — or even thought about — Summer.

"Ew!"

"What?"

"You thought about me while you were experimenting in the shower? God, Cohen, be more of a perv."

Ryan leaned over to Summer and grinned. "Bet you a thousand dollars he still does."

Seth looked from one to the other, completely aghast. "You guys, my parents are *right there*."

Seth turned bright red, about to die of embarrassment. He blinked a bunch of times, not sure how to salvage the situation, when Marissa kindly came to his rescue.

"I've never seen *Eyes Wide Shut*," she said. "But I hear it's pretty graphic. You must have been completely freaked out."

Maybe he could leave, Seth thought. Maybe he could go catch the end of *The Mummy*. Or use what was left of Sandy's money to play video games in the lobby. Or even just walk around outside in the sunshine. Because he honestly thought that if he had to watch one more second of the action onscreen, he would start shrieking.

He would have left a long time ago, but he didn't want his friends to make fun of him or think he was weird. He already was hated and made fun of by everyone in school — he didn't think he could take it if sailing class was ruined for him, too. But then he realized he wasn't the only one not enjoying the movie.

He had been avoiding looking at the other boys so they wouldn't see how uncomfortable the sex onscreen made him. But then he happened to glance over at Marc and saw that he was cowering in his seat with his hands over his eyes, watching the film through his fingers.

Thank god. He nudged Marc with his elbow. "You wanna go?" he whispered. Marc nodded and passed the message along to Lonnie, who shot out of his seat like it was on fire. Even Pete seemed relieved to make his escape.

They burst out of the doors and immediately started giggling.

"Did you see that?!" Lonnie exclaimed, stating the obvious.

"I never want to even look at a girl again!" Marc said.

"I bet Molly does that with her boyfriend," Pete said. Molly was their sailing instructor and a source of much admiration and gossip among the boys in the class.

"Gross!" The boys fell all over themselves with laughter, but then quieted down instantly when the theater manager, a chubby, mean-looking man in a too-tight sweater vest hurried over to them.

"Did you boys just come out of that theater?" he thundered, pointing at the door they had just exited.

Lonnie let out a little squeak of terror.

"We saw *The Mummy*," Pete said.

The manager got all puffy and red. "Don't lie to me!" he scolded. "I saw you come out."

"We're sorry," Seth said in a small voice. "But *Star Wars* was sold out."

The manager didn't seem impressed by this explanation. "Where are your parents?"

"My dad's coming to pick us up," Seth said, his voice barely a whisper now. "He'll be here when *Star Wars* ends."

"I think we better give your parents a call and have them come get you now," the manager said.

"I was so scared you were going to yell at me in front of those guys," Seth said with a small smile. "I remember sitting there trying to teach myself the Jedi mind trick in the twenty minutes it took for you to get there." He waved his hand like Obi-Wan. "*You are not mad at Seth,*" he commanded in his best Jedi voice.

"I wasn't angry to begin with," Sandy said. "I remember sneaking into *The Exorcist* when I was about the age you were."

"Did you get caught?" Ryan asked.

"No, but I almost wish I had! I was terrified for months after that — I had to sleep with my bedroom light on and couldn't tell my mom why."

"I bet the Nana would have understood," Seth said.

"That's a bet you'd lose," Sandy said ruefully. "But no, I wasn't mad about that birthday. Your birthday the following year, on the other hand, made me so furious you're lucky you're not *still* grounded. . . ."

Ever since Seth and Sandy had finished the boat that they'd refurbished together, Seth had been dying to sail it by himself. Every time he brought up the subject with his father, however, Sandy told him, "When you're older," without ever giving any indication of exactly how old "older" was.

By the time he turned eleven, Seth decided he was old enough. He'd been going to sailing camp for six years and could handle a boat better than most of the grown-ups he knew, many of whom had boats of their own. He'd even signed up to take the sailor certification test — how was he supposed to pass it if he never even had a chance to practice? He pled his case to his parents, but Sandy still said no. Seth was angry and frustrated, but there was nothing he could do about it.

This year, in lieu of a birthday party, Seth had asked Sandy if they could go to ComiCon, which was being held in San Diego that weekend. He'd been dreaming of attending the giant comic book convention ever since he could remember, but this was the first time that Sandy had agreed to take him. They decided to make a day of it — Sandy bought tickets for that afternoon, and they were going to stop at

Seth's favorite restaurant, a lobster shack on Laguna Beach, to have lunch on the way.

It sounded like a dream afternoon, but Seth had something he wanted to do first.

The morning of his birthday, Seth woke up while it was still dark out and silently got dressed. He let himself out of the house and skateboarded down to the marina. He was determined to prove to himself, if not to his dad, that he was old enough — and good enough — to handle the boat alone.

"Didn't you know that Sandy and Kirsten would freak when they found you were gone?" Ryan asked.

"I thought of that," Seth said, "so I left a note."

"A note saying he went to Marissa's house to do homework," Kirsten elaborated. "At six A.M. On a Sunday. On his birthday."

"Thanks for including me in your lie," Marissa piped up.

"Cohen! Don't you know how to create an alibi if you're going to lie to your parents?" Summer said. "It's a three-step process." She counted each step off on her fingers. "Invent a plausible excuse. Synchronize stories with your 'beard.' Develop a game plan to handle phone calls, accidental sightings, and other dangers of discovery."

Summer started to say more, then caught the look Sandy and Kirsten exchanged. "Not that I'd ever do that," she trailed off, blushing.

"Well, even if he had gotten Marissa to go along with the lie" — Kirsten started, causing Marissa to glare at Seth again — "it was about the most *implausible* excuse I'd ever heard."

"Seriously," Sandy agreed. "I'd have believed it more if he'd said he'd gone for tryouts for the water polo team!"

"I'll remember that for next time," Seth informed them.

Seth steered the little boat away from the marina with no problem at all. He decided he would just circle the harbor once, to show he could handle the skiff, then head back to the dock and be home before anyone noticed he was gone.

The water was smooth and placid, with a slight northerly wind luffing the sails, so Seth shifted the ballast forward to propel the boat out into the middle of the harbor.

He trimmed the sail so the wind was running abaft the beam, then leaned back against the mainsail, his eyes shut, enjoying the warmth of the rising sun on his face and the feeling of pride and accomplishment he had from handling the boat so expertly.

For a moment, he lost himself in a fantasy: He saw himself older, cooler, with a boat of his own, a pretty girl — Summer? — sitting on the stern as he sailed somewhere warm and exotic. Tahiti, maybe. Where the two of them would spend their days splashing in the surf, their nights together under the stars . . .

In his fantasy, Seth had just kissed Summer and was trying to figure out what to do with her next, when a spray of water doused him, snapping him back to reality.

In an instant, Seth realized that he must have had his eyes shut longer than he thought — the wind had carried the boat out of the harbor toward the open sea, where the water was choppier and the sails harder to handle.

Seth cursed under his breath — a good sailor always pays attention to his vessel and the water — but he didn't panic. If there was one area where Seth had confidence, it was that he knew his way around a boat. He decided his best course of action would be to open the boat up and run ahead of the wind, turning the boat in a wide circle that would point him back toward the marina.

He pulled on the rudder, aiming the prow of the boat toward the entrance to the harbor, but the rough water made steering harder than he'd ever felt it. Seth tried to haul the boat up, but the wind caught the sail, jibbing it in the wrong direction, and the boat shot forward, farther out toward open water.

Okay, this was a problem, Seth realized, but he took a deep breath and forced himself to relax. He wasn't going to drown, and even in heavy seas, he knew he could keep the boat from capsizing. As long as he kept his head and did exactly what he had learned in class, he'd be able to get back to the marina with no problems.

Seth studied the water, looking for clues to help him determine the best way to guide the boat. The waves were getting more tempestuous, slapping hard against the side of his skiff, and Seth anxiously scanned the sky for any sign of an approaching storm. While he was confident he could handle the boat on relatively calm water, he did not want to get caught in a squall.

He fastened the straps of his life jacket, which he'd been wearing loose, slung around his neck the way the cool teenagers who crewed on the yachts at the marina wore theirs, and took up position by the boom. He slowly pushed the helm leeward, until the sails began to tremble. Seth held it steady and reached for the rudder again. If he headed toward the open ocean, he should be able to angle the rudder against the current to push him back to shore.

And to his delight, it worked! The small craft began moving in the lazy trajectory he had coursed, and Seth couldn't resist giving himself a mental pat on the back.

This is the way sailors used to navigate, Seth told himself. *This is the way sailing is supposed to be.* He relaxed again against the mainsail, but this time kept his eyes open and alert. He wouldn't be blowing out the candles on his cake until later that day but made his birthday wish anyway. *I wish I could come sailing at night. I wish I could navigate by the stars.*

A larger, motorized ship was heading toward him, so Seth adjusted the rudder enough to pass by the other boat without throwing himself off course, but the motorboat shifted course, too, and was heading straight toward him.

Seth shaded his eyes with one hand, straining to see the other vessel, and realized with a start that it was a Coast Guard rescue boat. One of the officers on the ship shouted for Seth to drop sail, so Seth brought his boat to a halt and waited while the rescue boat pulled up alongside him.

"Seth Cohen?" the officer asked, swinging himself onboard without asking or waiting for permission.

"Yes," Seth answered miserably. This meant his parents knew he'd taken the boat, and that meant he was in big trouble.

"Lot of people looking for you," the officer said, gazing

around the deck to make sure everything was in order and Seth wasn't hurt or in danger. The officer had the sort of weatherbeaten, salty look that only true seamen could pull off. You could tell just from looking at him that this guy could sail anything, anywhere, in any weather. Seth hoped he would look like that one day. He'd settle for looking *half* as at home on a boat as the officer did.

"I went farther out than I had planned," Seth explained, "but I was on my way back."

"Well, we'll get you back quicker. Come aboard our boat, and we'll tow your skiff back to the dock for you."

"But I can do it myself," Seth protested.

The officer shook his head. "Let's go," he said, putting a hand on Seth's shoulder and gently guiding him over to the Coast Guard boat.

Other officers were tying a tow line to Seth's boat, and in no time at all they were chugging back toward the marina.

Seth looked out over the water, angry and disappointed. He'd been doing a great job. He could handle the boat alone. He certainly didn't need to be rescued, like some landlubber who didn't know a jib from a keel. It was — well, it was humiliating.

But as they got closer to the marina and Seth could see his parents standing on the dock waiting for him, his bitterness turned to dread. He was not looking forward to stepping ashore and having to face them. He knew he'd be lucky to ever get to go sailing again, after they got through with him.

As they pulled into the lock, Seth straightened up and

threw his shoulders back. He'd proven to himself that he was grown up enough to take the boat out alone; he might as well take his punishment like a grown-up as well.

One of the officers tossed a rope to people on deck, and the officer who had talked to Seth earlier came over to stand next to him.

"Those your parents?"

Seth nodded.

"They look pretty worried."

Seth shrugged. "I guess," he mumbled.

The officer studied him for a minute, then grinned. "They didn't need to," he told Seth, "'cause you can really handle a boat."

And despite the trouble he was in, Seth stepped onto dry land feeling happier than he could ever remember. He knew he probably wouldn't be getting the usual cache of gifts from his parents now, but that didn't matter. The Coast Guard officer had already given him the best present he could want.

THE OC

2001

"But — that's a happy story," Summer said.

Seth looked at her in disbelief. "Were you even listening?"

"But you ended up with all that high self-esteem," Marissa said. "Who cares if you had to be towed into the marina? You ended up with totally good self-esteem."

"Yeah, for about thirty seconds, until my parents got ahold of me," Seth conceded.

"You guys were pretty mad, huh?" Ryan asked Sandy and Kirsten.

"You don't even want to know," Sandy said.

Kirsten nodded. "When he wasn't in his room, and then we found the boat missing — well, I can't tell you the thoughts that went through my mind."

"Eaten by sharks?" Seth guessed. "Kidnapped by pirates? Capsized on a desert island?"

Kirsten shot him a look. "If you think you're being funny —" she said.

Seth laughed. "Come on. It was *years* ago. And I was fine. Besides, I had only gotten a few hundred yards from the harbor. It's not like I was trapped in a riptide and being whisked toward China."

"You could have been sucked into a whirlpool, though," Ryan said, "or swallowed whole by a whale."

"You know," Seth said, "that's something I've always wondered about. If you get swallowed by a whale, would you die? Or could you somehow live through it?"

"What, like Pinocchio's father?" Summer asked.

"No, but if you get swallowed all in one piece, couldn't they conceivably cut open the whale and get you back out?"

"I think whales have little teeth that would chomp you up," Marissa said. "Or else you'd drown. Or dissolve in the stomach acids."

"I think you'd be squished when it tried to blow you out of its blowhole," Ryan said.

"You'd die before the whale even swallowed you," Sandy told them. "You'd see it opening its giant mouth to eat you and drop dead of a heart attack on the spot."

Everyone laughed except for Kirsten, who was looking mutinously at her husband. "*Someone* won't need to worry about whales because *someone*'s about to be grounded."

Seth groaned and rolled his eyes. "You already grounded me for practically an entire year because of taking the boat — there's got to be a statute of limitations on punishments, right, Dad?"

"That's actually double jeopardy," Sandy said. "Can't be tried for the same crime twice." Then, before Kirsten could open her mouth, he hastily added, "Not that you wouldn't deserve it. That was a very bad thing you did."

"Well, I paid the price," Seth said. "On top of the grounding, no presents, no cake, and worst of all, no ComiCon."

"No ComiCon? I thought you were punishing him?" Summer remarked to Kirsten, who grinned.

"Oh, I got punishment enough on my next birthday, when I finally did make it to the comics convention," Seth told them.

Seth stood rooted to the floor at the entrance to the civic arena where ComiCon 2001 was being held, drinking in the amazing sight before him. Never in his twelve years on Earth had Seth seen such a wonderful abundance of things he liked. The whole auditorium was bursting with booths and kiosks and displays of every comic he could imagine, plus talks and demonstrations given by his favorite artists and writers. It was sheer heaven, and Seth was going to experience everything ComiCon had to offer.

Sandy had sprung for the collector's edition guide to the event, and Seth thumbed through it, so eager to get started he was about to burst.

There was a master class in drawing being offered by the editors at Marvel, a live-action performance of *New Mutants 216*, and — oh my god, Seth couldn't believe it — an appearance by the godfather himself, Stan Lee!

Seth shot off to find the room where Stan Lee would be speaking and signing autographs, and Sandy rushed to keep up.

He got to the room mentioned in the brochure, but found it empty, except for a hippie janitor who was setting up chairs.

"Is this where Stan Lee is going to be?" Seth asked breathlessly.

"In, like, two hours," the janitor told him.

"We should wait," Seth told his dad, "so we can get good seats."

"Why don't we take a walk around first?" Sandy suggested. "We'll make sure we're back in plenty of time."

Seth thought this sounded like an excellent idea — as much as he wanted to meet Stan Lee, he also couldn't wait to check out the rest of the conventions offerings.

Together, Seth and Sandy explored the exhibits. Seth bought more comics than he could imagine reading in a year, and Sandy finally purchased an X-Men Rogue tote bag just to carry them all.

They had reached the far end of the arena before Seth even thought to wonder how much time had passed. Sandy glanced at his watch — they had twenty minutes to get back to the room to see Stan Lee.

They picked up the pace, not bothering to stop for a second look at some of the booths they passed, although Seth made a mental note of what looked interesting so they could come back and check it out later.

They got back to the room with five minutes to spare and were surprised to see it empty! The same janitor told them that because so many people had shown up, they moved the talk to a larger hall, on the other side of the building.

Seth and Sandy raced to get to the new location but were too late. The hall was full, and the doors were closed — they couldn't even get in to stand in the back.

Seth was disappointed, so Sandy bought him a cherry sno-cone to cheer him up. But as they turned to go see more of the exhibits, Seth stopped, unable to believe his good fortune. Stan Lee was hurrying toward them with another man, late for the speech he was supposed to give!

"Dad! It's him!" Seth said happily. "I'm going to get his autograph!"

Seth darted out in front of his hero, promptly colliding with the man with Lee, who tripped over the smaller boy, and getting bright red sno-cone liquid all over Stan Lee's shirt and pants when he fell.

Seth picked himself up from the ground, a little dusty but barely noticing it because he was so thrilled to be face-to-face with Stan Lee. The man with Lee, on the other hand, was less pleased.

"Why don't you watch where you're going, you stupid little —"

"He yelled at you?" Summer asked, shocked. "But he was the one who bumped into you."

"I know, and I nearly knocked him down again myself," Sandy said.

"Did you hit Stan Lee's handler?" Ryan asked, sounding impressed despite himself.

"No, but I made him apologize, and Stan Lee was nice enough to give Seth an autograph," Sandy said.

"And buy me a new sno-cone!" Seth chimed in.

Everybody laughed, and as he looked around at his friends' and parents' smiling faces, Seth realized with a start that he'd been talking — and happily — about his birthday for nearly two hours, and it wasn't the nightmare he'd expected.

Usually Seth refused to so much as mention his birthday to anyone, but somehow, safe in the knowledge that his friends really did like him — that *Summer* liked him — Seth found these reminiscences tolerable, if not downright enjoyable. Maybe the Curse of the Cohen was losing its power over him. Then again —

"Tell us about the year after that," Summer said.

— maybe the curse was just picking up steam. . . .

THE

2002

"Ah, 2002, another prophetic year," Seth said. He gazed around at his friends, one eyebrow raised. "Anyone care to guess what happened on May sixteenth, 2002?"

They looked back at him, their faces blank, until finally Ryan raised a finger. "Could that be the date they released the next *Star Wars*?" he guessed lazily.

Seth clapped his hands. "Exactly. *Attack of the Clones* came out, and this time I was prepared."

"Absolutely not," Kirsten said, putting her foot down both literally and figuratively.

"But Mom," Seth wheedled, "the only way to get the good seats is to camp out overnight in front of the theater."

"Then you'll have to settle for bad seats," Kirsten said firmly.

Seth was determined not to have a repeat of the last *Star Wars* experience. He was going to spend his birthday at the opening night of the movie — and he was going to do it alone.

"You had to go to the movies alone on your birthday?" Summer asked. "That's so sad."

"No, it's not," Seth told her, "because I didn't *have* to go alone; I *chose* to go alone."

"Of course you did," Summer said sympathetically, giving his hand a little squeeze.

"I did!"

"Are you sure you don't want your mother and me to come with you?" Sandy asked. He was sitting on Seth's bed, watching his son put on the costume he had made for the big premiere. "We could stop for ice cream afterward."

"Really, Dad, I'd prefer to go by myself," Seth said for the millionth time. He wasn't sure how he could better explain that he'd rather go alone and let himself be completely absorbed by the spectacle than go with someone he knew wasn't totally into it. He wanted to be able to just relax and enjoy the movie without the person next to him shifting around in his seat and rolling his eyes and checking his watch every five minutes.

"I don't do that," Sandy said.

Both Seth and Kirsten burst out laughing. "Honey, you're the *worst* when you don't like the movie."

"I am not," Sandy said, offended.

"Come on. When we saw *Notting Hill*, you sighed so much I thought you were going for the world record."

"But *Notting Hill* was a terrible movie," Sandy said.

112

"I liked *Notting Hill*," Marissa protested.

"Me, too," Summer chimed in. "'I'm just a girl, looking at a boy, asking him to love me,'" she quoted.

Sandy sighed and rolled his eyes.

"Ha!" Seth said. "You see? Besides, when I got to the theater, I realized I wasn't actually alone. . . ."

Seth clambered out of the car, being careful not to mess up the ears on his outfit. After much consideration, he had decided to come to the movie dressed as Jar Jar Binks. While arguably the worst character in the entire *Star Wars* franchise, Seth thought it would be funny to show up dressed as him. Or if not funny, at least ironic. Besides, he had long since outgrown his Boba Fett costume, and it seemed a little too *much* to make another one.

Kirsten told him she'd be back to pick him up after the movie and drove away, tooting the horn twice to say good-bye. Seth turned and started into the theater, clutching his ticket tightly. He had a moment of panic — what if this time nobody dressed up for the movie, like they had for *The Phantom Menace* — but as soon as he got inside, he realized he needn't have worried.

The lobby was packed with people in costume — it seemed like more people than not were carrying light-sabers or had their hair rolled up into two Princess Leia doughnuts, and assorted Darth Vaders and Chewbaccas rubbed elbows with storm troopers, Ewoks, and sand people. Seth noted with satisfaction that he was the only Jar Jar Binks in sight, and even as he crossed to the line of ticket holders waiting to go into the theater, people were smiling at him and saying hi.

And once he was inside the theater, safely sitting dead center, ten rows back . . .

"A seat I *never* would have gotten if I hadn't been alone, by the way."

. . . once he was seated, Seth was amazed by the real feeling of camaraderie and acceptance in the audience. Suddenly it didn't matter that he didn't have any friends to go see the movie with — he found a theater full of friends once he was there.

Seth loved the movie, and when it ended, he didn't want to leave. He'd have been happy to hang out in the theater all night, trading *Star Wars* trivia and rehashing the movie with the other costumed aficionados. Still, he knew his mom would be waiting, so he finally, regretfully, made his way out to the lobby, a smile still on his face.

He ducked into the men's room, his costume proving to be more of a hindrance than he'd imagined — why hadn't he thought to give Jar Jar a fly? — and on his way out, who did he see but Summer, walking through the lobby with a gaggle of girlfriends.

"Oh, no," Summer said. "Another story about me ruining your birthday."

Seth decided to press his luck. He was in high spirits, still buzzing from the hit his costume had been and the fun, social atmosphere of the theater. Besides, if Summer had come to opening night of *Star Wars*, too, she'd appreciate how he was dressed. Not to mention that that would make her more perfect than Seth had even dared to dream.

He boldly stepped into her path, and she and her friends stopped when they saw him.

"Hello, ladies," Seth said. "Seeing the new *Star Wars?*"

Liesl, a dim girl in their class at Harbor, shook her head. "We just saw *My Big Fat Greek Wedding*. It was so funny. What did you see?"

Seth glanced down at his costume. "*Star Wars*," he told Liesl.

The other girls laughed and started to walk away. Encouraged, Seth gave Summer his best smile. "Bye, Summer."

"Bye," she answered, and brushed past him.

Seth's heart leaped. Summer had spoken to him! She knew who he was, or at least that he existed! He couldn't stop the grin from spreading over his face. He saw his mom's car pulling up to the curb and started toward it.

But the instant he was past the group of girls, they burst into laughter and he heard Summer say, "What a *geek!*" and his whole birthday was ruined.

"Okay, that's it," Summer said, shoving her stool back from the counter and standing up. "I can't take hearing any more of these stories. I'm sorry I was mean to you, but what's done is done, and there's nothing I can do. I'm not Spider-Man; I can't turn back time."

"Superman," Seth said.

"What?" Summer asked, annoyed.

"Superman was the one who could turn back time, by flying in reverse around the Earth. Spider-Man just climbed things."

"I don't care!" Summer shouted. "I was a monster to you. No wonder you hate your birthday. I'm surprised you don't hate *me*, too."

"I don't hate you!" Seth said, shocked. It was crazy, but it was almost like Summer then and Summer now were two totally different people. Or maybe *he* was the one who had changed.

"You're certainly not the first person ever to call Seth a geek," Marissa comforted her friend.

"And it seems to me like in most of these stories, the only person responsible for Seth being unhappy — is Seth," Kirsten added.

Summer thought about it. "I guess it *isn't* my fault that he dressed up like Jar Jar Binks," she decided. "Honestly, he was just asking for it, going around in public like that."

"Hey," Seth said, peeved.

"And the whole first grade-thing, where he blamed me after he ate all those cupcakes? I didn't tell him to be such a pig," Summer realized.

"Wait a minute," Seth said. "I'm not blaming you, at least not completely, for messing up my birthdays, but I certainly didn't *try* to have such a lousy time."

"What about the next year?" Sandy said. "Whose fault was that?"

Seth thought about it. "I'm going to have to go with Summer again."

"Cohen!"

Seth held up his hands. "What can I say? It's true."

"No it's not," Sandy corrected him. "If you had come out with your mother and me as planned, you would have had a terrific evening."

"You're right," Seth said, "and I just want to apologize again for my behavior that day."

Kirsten had pretty much accepted the fact that she wasn't going to get to plan any more birthday parties for Seth. At least not traditional ones, with noisemakers and silly games and lots of guests. But there was no reason she couldn't plan a family party that would be every bit as fun.

After calling in every favor and working every angle she had, Kirsten managed to score tickets to the touring company of *The Producers,* which was doing a limited engagement in Los Angeles. That and dinner at Nate 'n Al would make for an evening to remember. Kirsten thought about keeping the plans a secret, but Seth worried so incessantly that she was organizing some sort of forced social event with his peers that she finally broke down and told him what she had in store.

Seth couldn't wait. He'd watched the movie version of the original *The Producers* so many times that he wore out the tape. And Nate 'n Al was one of the few places Seth had ever been where *everyone* talked and acted like grizzled old Jewish men, not just him.

Seth was happy enough just to have something to do that evening. The Harbor School talent show was being held that same evening, and while Seth would never in a million years actually attend an event as peppy and school-spirited as a talent show, the idea of sitting home alone on his birthday while everyone else at school was out having fun together was a little hard to swallow. Even if, as Seth suspected, that was the case more nights than not.

The big day finally arrived. After school, Seth was in his driveway, practicing his K-grind on his skateboard and waiting for his parents to get home from work so they could leave for Los Angeles, when he saw Marissa and Summer come out of her house, dressed up so sexily he fell off his skateboard.

They were both wearing halter tops and Daisy Duke shorts, and teetered toward Julie Cooper's car on heels so high it was a miracle they could balance at all. Summer got into the car and slammed the door, but Marissa noticed Seth watching and lifted a hand in a half-wave.

"Where are you going?" Seth called over to her, unable to contain himself.

"We're doing an act in the talent show," Marissa told him. "Lip-synching 'Jenny from the Block.'"

"Coop!" Summer hung her head out the window, totally impatient. "Come on! We're going to be late."

Marissa got into the car, and Seth stared after it until it had rolled out of sight. He was pretty much the opposite of a J. Lo fan, but he did enjoy watching her videos once in a while, solely for the way she looked dancing. The thought of Summer doing those moves . . . Summer in those tiny shorts grooving like J. Lo in the video . . . Seth realized he wasn't breathing and gulped in air, unsteady on his feet.

He had to go to the talent show. Even if it was just for the beginning, but that sight was something he just couldn't miss. Only . . .

The talent show started at seven. *The Producers* started at eight. There was no way he'd make it back in time. Even if Summer was the very first act in the show, he'd be cutting it close.

Seth bit his lip, torn.

Maybe he could just swing by the school to sneak another peek at Summer in that outfit, then leave the rest of it up to his imagination. He'd gotten pretty good at that anyway, after all. And that way he'd be back in plenty of time to get to L.A. It was win-win.

His mind made up, Seth raced inside to leave a note for his parents. *Gone to the talent show @ school,* he scrawled on a sheet of notepaper. *Back soon.* He placed the note on the refrigerator where his parents would be sure to see it, then grabbed his skateboard and headed out the door.

"What happened?" Summer asked. "Did you guys not see the note?"

"Oh, we saw it," Sandy answered grimly.

"Even if we couldn't believe it," Kirsten added, her voice tight.

Seth got to the school and looked around for Summer. It seemed like every single student at Harbor had shown up for the event, along with their parents, siblings, and various friends. In short, the place was packed, and Seth had no idea how he was going to find Summer in the crowd.

He headed toward the backstage area in the auditorium, but one of the teachers who was monitoring the area stopped him. Only students actually performing were allowed backstage — if he wanted to see someone, he'd have to wait until their performance, same as everyone else.

Seth checked his watch, frustrated. If he had any hopes of making it home on time, he had to leave that minute. But as he was headed toward the exit, the door to the backstage swung open as one of the other performers went in, and in the brief gap he caught a glimpse of Summer, reapplying lipstick in a mirror, her lips pursed as she slid the crimson gloss over them, and any thought of leaving vanished from his mind.

"You know," Kirsten remarked, "those tickets were two hundred dollars apiece."

Sandy whistled, impressed. "Wow. And how many phone calls did you say you had to make to get them?"

"I stopped counting at two dozen," she answered.

Seth sighed. "How many times am I going to have to apologize for skipping that play?" he asked.

Kirsten and Sandy looked at each other, considering. "We'll let you know."

Summer's act was fuel for a lifetime of fantasies for Seth. Summer, Marissa, and three other girls did a perfectly synchronized routine, somehow managing to look both sultry and innocent at the same time. As it was ending, Seth ran out into the hall. He hoped he could intercept Summer to tell her how much he liked the act, then beat it home, with luck in time to make it to the *Producers* second act.

He positioned himself by the water fountain, pasting a friendly grin on his face when he saw the girls rushing down the hall, all of them chattering away a mile a minute. Summer was on the end closest to him, which seemed like a birthday present in itself, and as she brushed past him, he reached out a tentative hand to touch her arm.

"Great act, Summer!" he said in a voice that was a little too boisterous to fully disguise how nervous just being in her presence made him.

Summer glanced over to see who was talking to her, and her face, which had a split second earlier been animated and beaming, went flat when she saw him. It was like she was looking at a complete stranger — no, it was worse, it was like she was looking at a wall. There was no spark of recognition, no register of emotion — she didn't even look *annoyed* at his intrusion. It was like he didn't exist at all.

The next moment, a gang of jerks from the water polo team had materialized a ways down the hall, and as Summer turned toward them, away from Seth, the life rushed back into her face.

Seth felt like he'd been kicked in the stomach. How could she possibly have so little regard for him? He felt invisible. How in the world was he ever going to win her heart, if she didn't even know who he was?

"I figured out who you were pretty quick after that," Summer said, her eyes lighting up. Finally, a story she remembered — even if it wasn't necessarily the most dignified memory she had of him.

"What happened?" Ryan asked her.

She glanced at Seth — "Can I?"

He nodded, so Summer picked up with the story where he left off.

Summer leaned over the sink, splashing her face with lukewarm water, rinsing off the thick layer of garish makeup before it could clog up her pores. Liesl had already taken off her makeup and was bent over upside down, brushing her hair from the bottom up to try to give it more volume.

"That doesn't actually work," Summer told her, peeling off her false eyelashes. She was scrubbing at the glue that held them on, her face completely submerged under sudsy Kiehl's cleanser, when she heard the door being slammed opened and, all of a sudden, Liesl screamed!

What the hell?

"God! What happened?" she asked Liesl, who was giggling like mad now. Summer groped for a towel, squinting against the water running down her face.

"When the door opened, Ken Covey was standing outside, and I was flipped over, and he saw my butt!" Liesl explained. Ken Covey was the only freshman besides Luke to make the varsity water polo team. He was big and dumb the same way Liesl was little and dumb, and they'd been mutually crushing on each other for months.

Liesl threw her hairbrush in her purse and headed for the door. "I'm gonna go find him!"

Summer rolled her eyes, watching Liesl go, then finished

drying her face, noticing in the mirror a stray hair that ruined her otherwise-perfect eyebrows.

She reached into her makeup bag for her tweezers, when Marissa came into the bathroom, still in her J. Lo outfit.

"What's going on? Why did you scream?" Marissa asked, then stopped, looking at the tweezers in Summer's hand. "Oh. If you ice your eyebrows before you pluck them, it won't hurt so much."

Summer regarded Marissa calmly, then grabbed the offending hair and yanked, not even flinching. "I didn't scream; Liesl did."

"What did you do to her?"

"Nothing."

Marissa gave her a look — Summer was famous for sending other girls at school running for their lives. Summer looked back at her, her eyes flashing. "*Nothing.* She's nuts."

"Well, you are a little scary without mascara. . . ." Marissa said, cracking herself up.

"Shut up," Summer said, also starting to giggle. "At least I don't have to spend half my allowance on zit medication."

"Yeah, well, at least my hair doesn't look like a pony was chewing on it," Marissa answered. "At least I don't have hali-whatsis."

"Halitosis, loser," Summer said, laughing for real now, "and that's not what Luke said after last weekend."

"Hey —" Marissa started, but before she could think up a retort, the door slammed open again, and a gang of water polo players shoved a writhing and angry Seth into the bathroom.

124

"God, get out!" Summer yelled, grabbing the towel to cover herself, even though she was fully dressed in the tank top and jeans skirt she'd changed into.

"Sorry," Seth mumbled, shoving at the door. The jocks were evidently holding it shut from the other side, because Seth couldn't budge it.

Marissa started laughing, too, but managed to call through the door to Luke. "Hey, let go of the door, you guys."

The jocks let go all at once. Seth, who had been pushing with his shoulder as hard as he could, went tumbling out of the bathroom and landed on the floor.

He scrambled to his feet and threw a last backward glance at Summer, then fled down the hall, followed by the derisive laughter of the jock guys.

Summer watched him go, then turned to Marissa. "Does —"

"Wait! Stop!" Seth blurted out.

Everyone turned to stare at him, the words still hanging on Summer's lips. Seth shrugged sheepishly.

"I don't want to know what you said about me when I was gone," he said.

"It wasn't —" Summer started to say, but Seth shook his head.

"Even if it wasn't mean, or if you didn't say another word about me, can you just not tell us?" he said awkwardly.

"No problem," Summer said, her voice light. "Do you want to finish telling the story?"

"Nothing more to tell," Seth said. "I got home to a dark house and a message from Mom and Dad, written on the bottom of the note I had left them, saying that they had gone to the show without me."

Ryan tilted his head to one side. "Wait, so the next year I was living with you, right?"

"Yep," Sandy answered.

"So . . . how come no one ever brought up the fact that it was Seth's birthday? Were you guys still so mad from the previous year that you decided to stand *him* up?"

"Of course not," Kirsten said, distressed at the thought. "I would have loved to plan a party for him, especially since the two of you had become such good friends. But Seth wouldn't let me."

"He made us swear not to mention his birthday," Sandy said.

Ryan looked even more puzzled. "Why in the world would you do something like that?"

THE

2004

Seth checked the calendar and wrung his hands nervously. One week until his birthday, and he just knew something was going to go wrong.

For the first time in years, Seth actually could imagine his birthday turning out happily. Since Ryan had arrived to live with them, he actually had friends and — even more astounding — he had a *girlfriend*. It was all just too good to be true, but it was true, and because of that, Seth found himself paralyzed at the prospect of planning a birthday celebration. After all, since every time he got his hopes up that his birthday would end happily, he ended up crushed. He was afraid to even consider what sort of devastation would arise from a party that he went into thinking that this time nothing could go wrong.

Just the mere act of telling Ryan and Summer that it was his birthday was bound to set the wheels in motion for Summer breaking up with him, or Ryan deciding to move back to Chino, or some other, even more horrific thing that would ruin his birthday — and ruin his life. No, better to keep quiet about the whole sordid affair — that way his birthday would pass just like any other, ordinary, happy day.

But — Seth couldn't resist. He hadn't enjoyed his birthday in so long that he was itching to turn his luck around. It would be sad to pretend that it was just an ordinary day. There had to be a happy medium between jinxing it and skipping it altogether.

Finally, he hit on a plan. He would ask his friends to come over for dinner, *without telling them that it was his birthday.* That way, they would have a great evening, and at the end of it, when they were all feeling wonderful and the opportunity for disaster had passed, only then would he tell them the occasion. It was perfect.

And to make the evening even more special? Seth would cook the dinner himself. What better way to show his friends how much he appreciated them than with a delicious home-cooked meal?

It was sort of a crazy idea, Seth had to admit. After all, he was Kirsten's son, and she certainly hadn't passed along any genes for culinary skills. Sandy was a better cook, but even he had fallen into the habit of relying on takeout menus more than on any of the state-of-the-art appliances and fancy gadgets that sat, untouched, in their kitchen cupboards. And on the occasions when Sandy did cook, Seth was hardly tying on an apron and playing the role of sous-chef. So what made Seth think he was capable of pulling off a dinner for four? Honestly, it was because of Nigella.

Seth had been flipping through the channels a couple days earlier when he landed unexpectedly on the Food Network. He had never actually paused on this station for more than a few seconds, let alone watched an entire program, but he'd read an amusing review of *Iron Chef* online and figured he might as well check it out.

But *Iron Chef* wasn't on — *Nigella Bites* was, and she was preparing the most amazing-looking sandwich — just seeing it on the TV propelled Seth into the kitchen to scrounge one for himself. He settled back down with his snack and waited to change the channel until he saw what she prepared next.

The show made cooking look so easy and stress-free and *fun* that before he knew what he was doing, Seth was programming a season pass on TiVo and seriously considering dusting off their Cuisinart. Granted, he hadn't actually tried cooking anything yet, but he figured it shouldn't be too hard to go from watching to doing. And the thing he was going to make, he decided, was pasta with puttanesca sauce. Not that he cared so much for olives, but Nigella explained that *puttanesca* meant "whore pasta," because Italian hookers used to make it for the men they were entertaining out of anything they could find in their pantries, and with a story like that, Seth figured, how could anything go wrong?

His birthday fell on a Friday, so he assumed that if he waited until Wednesday to invite everyone, it would look casual enough that they wouldn't expect anything was up, but still be early enough that they wouldn't have made other plans.

Marissa, Summer, and Ryan all agreed to come to dinner without seeming to suspect anything out of the ordinary, although Ryan did mention how, seeing as he lived there, chances were he'd be eating dinner there that night regardless. Sandy and Kirsten had a party to attend for the Newport Group, but they promised to take him out on Saturday to make up for his birthday, which suited Seth fine. It would be fun having the house to themselves. Plus, that way no one would bother him while he was cooking, or try to help, when they clearly had no business being in the kitchen in the first place.

"I think he's talking about me," Kirsten remarked to no one in particular.

Thursday after school, Seth went shopping for the groceries. He didn't think he'd find some of the more esoteric ingredients at the local Ralph's Market, so he went to Sterling's Gourmet, an ultra-fancy, ridiculously overpriced shop he had never actually set foot in before.

The store was bustling, but Seth managed to find everything he needed, then made his way to the registers. The checkout line was a mob scene, with painfully thin Newport wives, teetering on their nine-hundred-dollar Manolos, all pestering the beleaguered stock boy for help finding virgin truffle oil and bittersweet Valrhona chocolates.

An older woman standing in line in front of Seth, Gucci sunglasses and Hèrmes scarf not quite concealing the evidence of a recent plastic surgery, grabbed the arm of a passing cashier.

"I'm looking for marinated artichokes," she rasped to the frightened-looking checkout girl.

The girl took a step backward, tugging her sleeve out of the woman's grasp. "Those *are* marinated artichokes," she said timidly, pointing to a small jar in the woman's basket.

"These are house brand," the woman said, outraged. "Don't you have anything more expensive?"

Seth let out a little snort of laughter, then quickly looked away so the woman wouldn't turn her wrath on him.

"Um, I think that's all we carry," the cashier stammered, taking tentative steps away from the woman.

"Nonsense," the woman said, picking up the jar and shaking it at the girl. "Do you know who my husband is? I want to speak to the manager!"

The cashier led the enraged woman away to the manager's office at the front of the store, and Seth let his laughter burst out.

He paid for his purchases, then headed home, convinced that the next day's dinner would break the Curse of the Cohen once and for all.

If Kirsten and Sandy thought it was odd that Seth didn't want them to mention his birthday in front of Ryan, they kept it to themselves.

After school, Ryan was helping Marissa hang decorations for a dance committee she was on, and Summer was meeting her father for coffee, so Seth, maintaining his casual attitude, told them all he'd see them at dinner and raced home to get started on his cooking.

He deftly minced three cloves of garlic, adding them to the bowl of chopped tomatoes, then sprinkled a few tablespoons of capers on top of that. Then he set the bowl aside and rummaged through a drawer looking for a pair of kitchen shears.

Hmmm. They didn't own kitchen shears. Seth left the kitchen and headed to his mom's office, where he nabbed her scissors. On his way back to the kitchen, he bumped into Ryan, who was storming his way to the pool house.

"Hey, are you okay?" Seth asked. Ryan's face was

clouded and grim, and Seth had a bad feeling about what was making him look that way.

"Theresa showed up at the school," Ryan said. "She's having some problems with Eddie and needs my help."

"But —" Seth wasn't sure what to say to this. "Is she okay?"

"Yeah, but I need to drive her back to Chino," Ryan said with a sigh.

"What, now?"

Ryan nodded. "Then I have to go see if Marissa is still talking to me. She freaked when I left with Theresa."

"Oh. Sure," Seth said, trying to mask his disappointment.

But Ryan noticed the expression on Seth's face. "Sorry. I know you wanted to have dinner —"

"It's fine," Seth said. God, he couldn't believe it. There was just no escaping the Curse of the Cohen. Now it was just going to be him and Summer, alone together. . . . Actually? Seth smiled as he headed back to the kitchen. Maybe things were working out for the best after all.

Seth turned up the volume on his new Bright Eyes CD, then picked up the can of anchovies that had been draining. Somehow you were supposed to cut the oily little fish up for the sauce, but he wasn't sure exactly how to do it. Did you cut off the hairy parts or what?

He grabbed the remote to the kitchen TV and rewound the *Nigella* show. Okay. He snipped the first anchovy in half, grimacing at the cracking sound its little bones made as he cut through it.

When the sauce was safely simmering, Seth headed up to his room to get changed. He hadn't been planning on getting dressed up at all, but now that it was just him and Summer he figured he might as well put on the dog a little bit.

He took a fast shower — she was due to arrive any minute, and their relationship was new enough that he didn't think she needed to see him in a towel and dripping — then got dressed and went back downstairs.

He set the dining room table using the heirloom china normally reserved for holidays and special occasions, and even lit a couple candles to put Summer in the mood for romance.

When everything was set, he glanced at his watch. Summer should have been there twenty minutes ago. The bag of fresh pasta was lying on the counter, waiting to be boiled, but he didn't want to put it in until Summer had arrived. He'd give her ten more minutes, then he'd call to see where she was.

Five minutes later, he couldn't wait any longer and picked up the phone.

"Hey, Summer, whatcha doing?" he said when she picked up.

"Hey, Cohen, I can't really talk right now," Summer told him.

Seth did his best to ignore the sinking feeling in his stomach. "Everything okay?"

"Sure, but I'm with my dad, and he thinks it's rude to use cell phones in restaurants."

Okay. "You sure have been getting coffee for a long time," he said, trying to keep his voice upbeat.

"There was a new place Dad wanted to try, so we decided to get dinner."

"I thought you were coming over here for dinner," he said, feeling like a whiny little kid.

"You don't mind, do you?" Summer asked. "I thought you said it was no big deal."

Seth fought back the lump in his throat. "Sure. I'll talk to you tomorrow."

"Bye."

Seth trudged back to the kitchen and stared at the damned puttanesca sauce boiling on the stove. He wanted to pick it up and hurl it against the wall. Instead he turned off the heat under the pan, ordered a pizza to be delivered, then headed into the living room to delete *Nigella* from their TiVo forever.

"If you'd told me it was your birthday instead of pretending that we were just going to be hanging out like usual, I would have shown up," Summer said, exasperated.

"Yeah, it's not fair for you to blame us because we didn't somehow magically divine that it was your birthday," Marissa agreed.

"How could you not know when my birthday is, after all those parties you came to?" Seth demanded.

Marissa blew out a frustrated breath. "That's ridiculous. You don't know when *my* birthday is."

"October second," Seth shot back at her. And before the others had time to respond, he pointed at Summer, then Ryan. "August twelfth, February eleventh."

The other kids looked at him, half-impressed, half-guilty.

"But I'm not *blaming* you," Seth continued patiently, "I'm just stating the facts. Which are that you all blew me off on my birthday."

Ryan sighed. "Is that why you didn't plan anything last year?"

"I did plan something last year," Seth told them, "and I'm sorry to say, you all let me down again."

Ryan, Marissa, and Summer looked at one another, confused. "What did you plan?" Summer asked.

"Six words," Seth told them, and held up his fingers to count off. "*Star Wars: Revenge of the Sith.*"

The other kids looked at one another and sighed. "Here we go again," Ryan muttered.

Seth wasn't going to make the same mistake this year he'd made last year. Or rather, he clarified, he was only going to make *part* of the same mistake.

He still believed that the only way to get through his birthday without the Curse of the Cohen showing up was to not tell anyone it was his birthday. On the other hand, he needed to stress to his friends how important it was to him that they all show up when he asked them to. Luckily, this year he had a reason that they couldn't help but respect. It was the opening of the final *Star Wars* movie, and he had tickets.

He announced to Summer, Ryan, and Marissa two weeks before the movie opened that it was *Very Important* to him that they all make attending it with him a priority, and gave them each daily reminders that he fully expected them to show up on time and eager for the show itself. Where they drew the line, however, was at wearing costumes.

"Come on," Seth pleaded. "There are four of us. We can go as Luke, Leia, Han, and Chewy from the original. It'll be perfect."

"Over my dead body," Summer said. "It's bad enough that you're going to make us go on a night when the theater will be full of dorks with light-sabers, but there's simply not enough money in the world to make me put on a costume and parade around Newport."

"Even if you're Leia?" Seth cajoled. "You'd look pretty hot in that white dress. . . ."

"Wait a minute," Marissa interrupted. "How come Summer gets to be Leia and not me?"

"Because . . . Summer's got dark hair, like the princess," Seth said as diplomatically as possible. "And you're tall, like the Wookiee."

"You want me to be Chewbacca?! Forget it," Marissa said.

Ryan gave Seth a sympathetic look. "Bad move. She was the only one of us who might have been willing to get dressed up with you."

"Not anymore I'm not," Marissa said.

Seth looked at Ryan, injured. "You'll dress up with me, though, right?"

Ryan gave Seth his blankest look by way of an answer.

"You won't? Oh, I can't believe this!" Seth said, throwing up his hands in defeat. "What if we go as Luke and Vader? I could rig up a fake hand, maybe, and you could cut it off . . . that'd be so cool."

"Seth."

"We could do that scene, you know, where he tells him

137

he's his father, and at the end of it, when I scream for Ben —"

"Seth."

"I'll let the hand topple, and — oh, this is going to be great —"

"*Seth!*"

Seth finally looked over at Ryan, who slowly shook his head.

Seth paused for a minute, while he tried to come up with an argument that might get his friends to get into the spirit of things and get dressed up with him, but finally realized it was futile.

"Spoilsports," he muttered, and stomped off to his room, to figure out what to do with the Wookiee costume he'd been working on.

Of course, when the big day arrived, he was just as glad that he hadn't knocked himself out making costumes for everybody. Because surprise, surprise, everybody backed out.

Ryan got a call from Trey, who needed his help and couldn't wait, and there was no way Ryan could say no.

Marissa didn't think Ryan should deal with his brother alone, so she mumbled "sorry" to Seth and followed Ryan out the door.

That left just Summer. She looked up at Seth, who was shrouded in a truly excellent Darth Maul outfit he'd made, and shook her head.

"Sorry, Cohen, but I just can't do it. Not with you dressed like that."

"But you knew all along I was planning on wearing a costume," Seth said, in a hopeless sort of voice. He should

138

have known, he thought, he should have seen this coming from a mile away.

"But I thought Marissa and Ryan would be with us," she explained, "as sort of a . . . buffer of cool."

Seth's eyes opened wide at the betrayal. "You were going to pretend Ryan was your date!" he accused, and was answered with a shrug, which he took to be an admission of guilt.

"I just can't see myself sitting next to you in public while you're wearing that — burka," Summer told him.

"I hate to keep repeating this," Summer said, "but if only you'd told us it was your birthday, I would have gone to the movie with you."

"Would you have dressed up like Princess Leia?" Seth asked.

"Of course not," Summer said, "but I wouldn't have made you change your costume."

"That's sweet, but I don't need your charity," Seth joked.

Summer blinked. "Cohen —"

Seth held up a hand to stop her. "I am perfectly capable of enjoying a movie whether you are there or not," he said archly.

Marissa gave him a pitying look. "Did you go by yourself again?"

"No," Seth said, "Dad went with me."

"That's right," Sandy said, "and I even dressed up."

"No way!" Ryan said, laughing. "Who did you go as?"

"I wore a pair of Spock ears."

Summer leaned over to Seth. "Isn't that the wrong galaxy?"

Seth shook his head ruefully. "Don't get me started."

Seth was really surprised at what a good time he had seeing the movie with his dad. It was so different from when he'd first tried to see *The Phantom Menace*. Back then, he'd been so desperate to show off his independence, he would have felt like a failure if Sandy had insisted on chaperoning. Of course if Sandy had come along, maybe Seth and his friends would have actually *seen* the movie.

And when he saw *Attack of the Clones*, Seth had been feeling so lonely and friendless that if Sandy had come along, he wouldn't have been able to enjoy the welcoming atmosphere of the crowd nearly as much as he had. With his father there watching, the warm acceptance of the audience would have only served to highlight just how alone Seth usually was.

But this time, for *Revenge of the Sith*, Seth made the happy discovery that he no longer had either of those negative feelings. He had friends, so he didn't depend on the audience's approval to make him feel like he belonged somewhere. And since he already knew how resilient and independent he was, Seth was able to relax and enjoy his father's company. It was simply more fun to see the movie with someone than alone.

If anything, the evening reminded Seth of when Sandy had taken him to see the revival of the original *Star Wars*, years before. Back then, he wasn't concerned with his image or popularity or dating or any of the other zillion tiny neuroses that shaped his personality. All that mattered to him then was the dark theater, the comfort of his dad sitting next to him, and the sheer absorption, from the first moment the Death Star appeared on the screen, in this other world of possibility —

"Geez, Melinda," Ryan interrupted, "are you getting residual checks from Hallmark?"

"What do you mean?" Seth asked, annoyed at being cut off mid-sentence.

"They weren't just father and son," Marissa intoned in her best "after-school-special" voice. "They were also . . . friends."

"God, you people are soulless," Seth said.

"Well —" Sandy said, scrunching up his face, "you were laying it on a bit thick there."

"Forgive me for trying to find some symbolism or meaningful through-line to my life," Seth complained.

"Duh," Summer told him. "The through-line is that because you're afraid to ask for what you really want, you're always disappointed by what you get."

"That's — I don't think that's it," Seth said.

But the others all shouted, "Yes, it is!"

"Just tell us what you want to do to celebrate your birthday and we'll do it," Kirsten said.

Seth shook his head, panic rising in his eyes. "I don't want to do anything," he said.

"Then why have we been talking about this for" — Summer glanced at her watch — "three hours?"

"I told you three hours ago I didn't want to celebrate!" Seth said. "The Curse of the Cohen —"

"Just think up what would make you happy, we'll do it, and the curse will be broken," Ryan said.

"Uh-uh." Seth set his face in a stubborn line. "Last year actually turned out pretty good — no matter how Hallmarky you guys found it. I think I'm going to let that one ride for a while."

The others looked at one another doubtfully. "So you really don't want us to do *anything* on Thursday?" Kirsten said.

"You can wish me a happy birthday," Seth told them, "then let the matter drop. *That's* what I'm asking for, and that's all I want."

"Fine," Sandy said, standing up and looking at his watch, too. "Whew, I gotta get some work done," he said, and headed out of the room, Kirsten right behind him.

Summer looked over at Marissa and noticed for the first time the shopping bags she had brought in with her. "Ooh, what'd you buy, Coop?" she asked.

"Come on, I'll show you," Marissa answered, and the girls picked up the bags and disappeared.

Ryan stood and stretched. He looked at Seth like he was going to say something, but then thought better of it and walked out of the room without another word.

And Seth was left alone in the kitchen. He got up and absentmindedly started clearing up the napkins and empty pizza boxes that were still cluttering the counter.

Well, he'd asked for everyone to ignore his birthday, and it looked like he was going to get what he asked for. But was that what he really wanted?

Seth looked down at the floor, unsure *what* he wanted anymore. Then he picked up the garbage bag and carried it out to the trash.

THE OC
2006

When Seth woke up on Thursday morning, he lay in bed for a minute before opening his eyes. *Let today be a good day*, he thought, making a silent birthday wish. He stretched out a foot, tentatively feeling for weight on the end of his bed where his parents traditionally piled his birthday presents. He didn't feel anything, so he cracked open an eye. There was nothing there.

Hmmm. Well, maybe this meant everybody was going to respect his request to ignore his birthday. That was the best present they could give him, right? Even though he had sort of been hoping for a new PSP game system. Still, it was better this way.

Seth got out of bed and threw on his clothes, then padded down the stairs to the kitchen. He assumed that since there were no presents, there probably also wasn't a surprise party waiting for him — and he was right.

Ryan and Sandy were seated at the counter, sipping coffee and chewing on bagels. Neither of

144

them looked up as Seth pulled a bagel out of the bag and deftly sliced it in half.

"Good morning," he said pointedly, shoving it into the toaster.

"Morning," Sandy said. "Happy birthday."

"Yeah," Ryan mumbled, spewing crumbs, "happy birthday."

"Thanks," Seth said, waiting for more. But Sandy and Ryan simply returned to the newspaper.

This was . . . kind of an anticlimax. Seth hated to admit it, but his feelings were hurt. Sure, he'd asked for this, but come on. Would it kill them to show a little enthusiasm? Luckily, Kirsten came into the kitchen just then, her hands hiding something.

"Happy birthday!" she said to Seth, giving him a guilty grin. "I know you wanted us to pretend like today was any other day, but I couldn't resist —"

"Mom, hey —" Seth started happily. "I actually was just thinking —" But before he could finish his sentence, she revealed her big surprise: a cinnamon bun with a single candle sticking out of it.

"I hope you don't mind my making a little fuss," Kirsten said.

She called this a fuss? "S'fine." Seth shrugged, then leaned over to the cinnamon bun.

He thought for a second about revising his earlier wish, asking the universe to bring him that PlayStation Portable, but that felt like a bit of a cheat, after all his complaining the day before. So Seth merely repeated his earlier wish — *let today be a good day* — and he blew out the candle.

School was the same letdown the morning had been. Marissa wished him a happy birthday when she saw him, and Summer said good morning and gave him a sexy kiss on the lips.

"Was that my present?" he asked her, hoping she would say that it was just the card, and he'd have to wait till they were alone together to unwrap the real thing, but Summer just shook her head.

"No party, no present," she told him, and sashayed away down the hall, leaving him frustrated, confused, and more than a little regretful about how he'd chosen to celebrate this day.

By the time the final bell rang, Seth was feeling pretty blue. Sure, it had been a basically good day, but that's how every day was. Today he wanted something special. Special without ending in tears. Was that asking so much?

But as Seth walked out to the student parking lot with Ryan, he decided it was silly to get down in the dumps about the way people were treating him, when he had brought it all on himself. He had the choice of whether to be miserable or not, and he realized with a shock that he was bringing the Cohen Curse down on himself. If he kept up this gloom-and-doom routine all day, he could mark this birthday down as a bust, same as all the others. No — if he wanted to have a happy birthday, all he needed to do was *be happy*, and the thing that would make him happiest of all? A trip to Newport Comics.

He asked Ryan if he'd like to come along, and

even though Ryan wasn't close to being as big a comic book fan as Seth was, he didn't hesitate to agree.

See? Seth told himself. *That's another present right there.*

The two boys spent well over an hour in the comics store, then Seth unloaded the check from the Nana on the latest couple editions of *Gotham Central*, then they headed back to the Cohens', Seth doing his best to convince himself he was having the best birthday ever.

They got home and let themselves in through the side door near the pool. The house was quiet, and Ryan looked at Seth. "Where is everybody? I thought your parents would be home by now."

Seth shrugged. *Of course* they'd be working late on his birthday. But — that wasn't looking on the sunnier side of things, so he forced his face into a smile. "If they don't get home soon, we can order dinner in."

Ryan shrugged too. "I guess." He looked at his friend, then grinned. "Hey, you wanna watch *Hellboy*?"

Seth's face brightened. "Really?" He'd made all his friends watch that movie so many times, they had boycotted even hearing the title ever again.

Look at that, Seth thought. *Another present.*

He headed toward the family room to start the DVD, Ryan following on his heels. Seth walked into the family room and flipped the light switch, and —

147

"Surprise!"

Seth stopped dead in his tracks, amazed at the sight before him.

The family room had been transformed into a Mexican bazaar, just like the one Sandy had described from his first birthday. There was a cake in the shape of a Matchbox car sitting on the coffee table, and Sandy, Marissa, and Kirsten were all holding brightly wrapped packages — and wearing pirate eye patches.

Seth laughed out loud, dazzled by the party his family had prepared for him. "You guys!" he said, smiling so big he thought his face would break. "What did you do?"

"We're breaking the Curse of the Cohen," Ryan said. He reached over and hit *play* on the stereo, and an Air Supply CD started playing.

"You were in on this?" Seth asked, genuinely surprised.

"I thought I was never going to get you out of that comic book store," Ryan said.

"Well, it's about time you did! Now you'll have to wait to open your presents until after we get home," Kirsten said, stepping forward to give her son a hug.

"Home from where?" Seth asked.

"We have reservations at Café Figaro for puttanesca," Sandy said, "then we're going sailing."

"But you have to open this one before we leave," Marissa said, and handed Seth a flat box.

He opened it, and two DVDs fell out — *The Producers* and *Eyes Wide Shut*.

Seth looked at the movies, overwhelmed. "What —" he started, unsure of the question he wanted to ask.

But Sandy knew the answer anyway. "We thought if we took all the bad things that have happened to you on your birthday and set them right, maybe we'd turn your luck around, and you'd have happy birthdays from here on out."

Seth's grin grew wider. This really was a perfect day. Except — there was one thing missing.

"Thanks so much, you guys," he said, "but where's Summer?"

Then he heard her voice. "I'm right here."

Seth turned around, and if he had been surprised before, now he was so astounded it was a miracle he didn't topple right over.

Summer was standing in front of him, dressed head to toe in Seth's old Jar Jar Binks outfit! It was the most hilarious, heartwarming thing he'd ever seen. And just when he thought it couldn't get any better, she held out her present to him: a cupcake with pink and purple sprinkles.

"Happy birthday, Cohen," she told him, her smile practically as big as his own.

He grinned and brought the cupcake to his mouth to take a bite, then stopped. "Did you touch this?" he teased. "Those look like fingerprints."

Summer laughed and playfully tapped his hand,

bashing the cupcake into his face so he got frosting smeared on his cheek.

Seth grabbed Summer and gave her a spectacular kiss, getting frosting all over her in the process.

Ryan, Marissa, Sandy, and Kirsten spontaneously broke into applause, thrilled that they were able to make Seth happy.

"Lifted, the Cohen Curse is," Marissa said in her best Yoda voice, and everyone started laughing, Seth loudest of all.

If it took a lifetime of bad birthdays to get to one this good, Seth thought, beaming at his friends and parents, *well, it was worth it.*

You Haven't LIVED The O.C.
Until You've Read More of The O.C.

WHAT HAPPENS WHEN RYAN AND SETH HEAD TO NEW YORK?

GO ON THE ADVENTURE IN *SPRING BREAK*.
AVAILABLE MARCH 2005

ON FAMILY VACATION, WHAT DOES SUMMER GET CHALLENGED TO DO BY A HOT GUY?

DROOL ABOUT IT IN *THE SUMMER OF SUMMER*
AVAILABLE JUNE 2005

WWW.SCHOLASTIC.COM

SCHOLASTIC

TM & © Warner Bros. Entertainment Inc. (s05)

You Haven't LIVED The O.C.

Until You've Read More of The O.C.

A STORY YOU *WON'T* SEE ON TV

THE O.C

Aury Wallington

Bait & Switch

WHAT HAPPENS WHEN THE GANG GOES ON A SCAVENGER HUNT?

JOIN THE RACE IN *BAIT AND SWITCH*

AVAILABLE SEPTEMBER 2005

WHAT'S STIRRING IN THE MANSIONS OF NEW PORT?

FIND OUT IN *'TWAS THE NIGHT BEFORE CHRISMUKKAH*

AVAILABLE DECEMBER 2005

A STORY YOU *WON'T* SEE ON TV.

THE O.C

by A. Van Suckle

'Twas the Night Before Chrismukkah

WWW.SCHOLASTIC.COM

SCHOLASTIC

TM & © Warner Bros. Entertainment Inc. (s05)